All she could think of was her daughter.

"Do you think..."

Her voice trailed, but Colby knew what she didn't ask. "I think Olivia is still alive," he said.

"How can you be sure?"

"Because they clearly want you alive as well—which, to be honest, is what has me more worried."

She nodded without pressing him. She knew that if the bullet they'd fired had been a real one, she would be dead.

That was when regular programming changed and the local TV news anchor came on-screen. According to the report, her nanny was dead. Then her picture was shown. "If you see this woman, contact local authorities immediately."

Regan's stomach felt like a boiling mass of acrid liquid. It was as if her life was now an overturned hourglass—each grain of sand taking minutes off not only her life but Olivia's, as well.

Her nanny was dead. If they could kill her so easily... what did that mean for her daughter?

Would any of them make it out alive?

Jordyn Redwood is a pediatric ER nurse by day, suspense novelist by night. She pursued her dream of becoming an author by first penning her medical thrillers *Proof*, *Poison* and *Peril*. Jordyn hosts *Redwood's Medical Edge*, a blog helping authors write medically accurate fiction. Living near the Rocky Mountains with her husband, two beautiful daughters and one crazy dog provides inspiration for her books and she loves to get email from her readers at jredwood1@gmail.com.

Books by Jordyn Redwood

Love Inspired Suspense

Fractured Memory
Taken Hostage

TAKEN HOSTAGE

JORDYN REDWOOD

Recycling programs for this product may not exist in your area.

ISBN-13: 978-0-373-67849-5

Taken Hostage

This edition published by arrangement with Love Inspired Books.

www.Harlequin.com

Printed in U.S.A.

And if one prevail against him, two shall withstand him;
and a threefold cord is not quickly broken.

–*Ecclesiastes* 4:12

For my friend and mentor Candace Calvert.
Thank you for taking me under your wing
and being a guiding light on my writing journey.

Acknowledgments

Thank you to everyone at Harlequin
for all the hard work you put into these books.
Special thanks to my editor, Emily Rodmell, for always
being available to answer my questions and offer
invaluable help during the writing and editing process.

Always a special thank-you to my friend and agent,
Greg Johnson. Hopefully some big things will happen
this year!

I couldn't do what I do without the support of my
amazing husband, James. If I have any ability to write
romance, it is because you show it to me every day in
both big and small ways. I'm the luckiest girl.

ONE

Ten bullets. Nine in the clip, one in the chamber. Checked twice.

That was what fugitive recovery officer Colby Waterson carried at all times to protect himself. Extra clips didn't matter because it was rare to have time to reload. Especially when working alone.

However, today was not about hunting fugitives from the law. Today was about helping save his sister Sam's life. Today was the day Colby Waterson was going to meet Dr. Regan Lockhart. The one woman…the only human being alive… who could save his sister from a brain tumor that had thus far refused to die at the hands of conventional medical therapy.

Colby thrummed the steering wheel of his crimson-red Ford F-250. Needles of anxiety wormed through his chest and his breakfast sat heavy in his gut. He glanced at his watch. If traffic kept this pace, he'd be on time.

As long as nothing happened. As if hearing his thoughts, the rains let loose, torrential and determined, momentarily obliterating his view of the road until he engaged his windshield wipers, which only moderately improved visibility.

I should have left earlier. Why did they schedule this meeting so early in the morning? It's a crime to be up before sunrise.

The roar of an engine drew Colby's attention out his driver's-side window as a black GMC Yukon flew past him and then squeezed in like a sardine between Colby and the blue Toyota Sequoia he'd been trailing.

What's the rush, big man? Want to make sure everyone sees your nice, shiny, new toy? Was the maneuver worth getting a whole car length ahead?

Colby eased back a few paces to increase the distance between him and the black SUV. As a bounty hunter, he was constantly on the lookout for trouble, no matter what his agenda for the day was. After all, good days often turned into the worst kind. *Like hearing your wife has cancer on the same day she tells you she's pregnant.* And then losing both his wife and unborn child within five months. The event that marked his life was over a decade ago yet still always felt like yesterday.

The black Yukon sped up and began riding the

bumper of the navy blue Sequoia. Heat spread in Colby's chest and he glared at the back of the driver's head between windshield wiper passes. There was no doubt—the guy was driving recklessly and the fresh onslaught of rain only provided a slippery surface for added danger. Hydroplaning was quickly becoming a risk. Trepidation caused Colby's flesh to prickle.

Seriously, what is your problem?

The driver of the Sequoia sensed the invasion and began to pick up speed. As the car pulled ahead, the driver was a black silhouette, but it appeared to be a woman. Now there were two cars increasing their speed on a rainy highway.

The Sequoia switched lanes to the right, into the slow lane.

And the Yukon immediately followed her instead of passing, nearly kissing her rear bumper to get in front of the car occupying the same space on the road.

Colby gripped the wheel in his hand, his heartbeat in his throat.

Something isn't right here. Whoever is driving that car is clearly after that woman.

Deciding the best action was to observe from a safer distance, Colby dropped back several car lengths and grabbed his phone. Getting the boys in blue seemed like the best option before someone got hurt.

Just as his thumb hit the nine for 9-1-1, the Yukon pressed ahead and slammed into the left rear bumper of the Sequoia, shoving the SUV a dizzying one-hundred-and-eighty degrees across three lanes of traffic. Colby's heart stalled as the Sequoia arced in front of him, the woman's hair flung to the side as her vehicle roared across the rainy road. Cars slammed on their brakes to avoid getting hit.

Colby instinctively knew exactly where the Sequoia was going to end up—on the shoulder of the fast lane, facing traffic. Colby braked hard and yanked his steering wheel left. The Sequoia struck the cement barrier and the woman disappeared from view. Colby punched his brakes, his heart hammering at the base of his throat, his bumper inches from the other SUV.

Without thinking, he released his seat belt and opened his door. It crashed into the divider after opening just a few inches. He scrambled to open the passenger door and that was when he saw two men shielded in black ski masks exit the Yukon with guns raised. Colby opened his glove box and grabbed his Glock, pushed open the door and half jumped, half fell out onto the road.

The loud pops of the two thugs firing their weapons sent Colby's mind reeling back to Iraq. He hunched down, squared his stance and fired two shots from his Glock above their heads, causing the two to retreat to their vehicle.

Eight defensive chances remained.

He raced to the Sequoia and opened the door. The woman was just righting herself, bringing her hand up to stem the flow of blood from a cut on her forehead. She'd hit her head on something. At the moment, Colby didn't care what it was. He simply wanted her out of the car and down on the ground.

Reaching over her lap, he disconnected her seat belt. She was disoriented, looking at him with a far-off, disconnected gaze.

"What…happened?"

"Ma'am, I need you out of this car. There are two men—"

Shots rang out and bullets punched holes into the navy blue paint. Colby turned and fired off three more shots to drive the black-clad men back to ground.

Eight. Seven. Six.

He then reached around the thin woman and muscled her out of her vehicle, settling her not-so-gently on the wet, black pavement. She stared up at him, her gray-green eyes distant, her styled red hair tangled.

That was when he recognized her. Dr. Regan Lockhart. The woman who was to save his sister.

Colby reached for his phone, which he normally kept in his back pocket, and remembered dropping it on his passenger seat. He glanced across the roadway. The only sound was the rain thrashing in his ears. His clothes were caked against his flesh. He couldn't see the two men but, if he had to guess, he'd say they were maneuvering to outflank him. Colby heard sirens in the distance but it only took a second to fire a kill shot.

What did these men want with a neurosurgeon?

Not sure his plan was the best but out of options, he grabbed her arm and pulled her up over his shoulder. He squared himself back to the black Yukon.

Five. Four.

Two more rounds gone from his arsenal, but hopefully worth the risk to provide cover. He scrambled to his vehicle. As he reached the front of his truck, a round punched into the hood. He yanked open the passenger door, threw the doctor unceremoniously into the well of the passenger seat and scrambled across into the driver's seat, reaching to pull the door closed, keeping his head as low as possible. His windshield shattered, spraying shards of safety glass over both of them. The showering crystals seemed to convince the woman to stay put.

He needed distance between them and these gunmen. He raised his Glock.

Three. Two.

At this point, he couldn't risk any more blind shots. The last bullet had to be saved for a close encounter. Colby threw his truck in Reverse and stomped on the gas pedal, praying that no one was behind him.

Dr. Regan Lockhart's ears rang from a combination of metal sheering against metal and the booms of guns firing. Her head pounded from slamming into the steering wheel and her normally logical thoughts swam in a sea of woodsy cologne and leather. The backward lurch of the truck caused her breakfast to roil in her stomach like sharks after chum. She pressed her hands into the gray-carpeted floor mat that was littered with glass and tried to lift her head up.

She felt a palm push at the back of her head. "Stay down!" a strong male voice ordered. Just as well, as the dizziness made it difficult to tell up from down at the moment and his hand on her head provided a steadying force.

What happened?

Sirens overwhelmed the ringing and her eardrums ached from the onslaught of honking horns. The truck jerked to a stop and the male occupant—the one who'd pulled her from her vehicle under a hail of bullets—jumped out. No longer hearing the sounds of shots being fired, Regan ever so slowly raised her head and found a vacuous hole where the windshield had been. She placed her arms on the black leather passenger seat now slick with rainwater, the glass tinkling musical notes as she brushed the shards off so she could push up without further cutting her hands.

Just as she was about to settle herself onto the seat, the passenger door opened and she got a good look at the stranger. He reached his hand out to her, his muscled arms visible through the buttoned-up shirt that clung to his chest from the rain.

"Can you move or should I help?" he asked.

She placed her quivering hand in his steady one. How was he not shaky from all that had happened? When both her feet hit the road, her legs withered, and he helped ease her gently onto the pavement, keeping his hand underneath her head until it, too, rested on a bed of gravel.

"Are you okay?" he asked.

"Who…are you?" Regan asked.

"Colby. Colby Waterson."

Waterson. Something pinged in Regan's memory. Inherently she knew that name was important.

"You need to stay down," Colby said, hovering

over her to keep the rain off her face. "The police are starting to canvass the area for the people who ran you off the road and tried to kill you."

Kill? Had she heard that right?

"An ambulance is on the way," Colby reassured her. "Do you want them to take you to Strang Memorial?"

So he did know her in some measure.

Regan pulled her hands up to her face and lightly tapped the wound at her forehead. Sticky—the time between blood freshly flowing and drying.

"You'll need stitches," he informed her. "Maybe a CT scan, but then again...you'll know best. You're the neurosurgeon and all."

Regan desperately needed this world to slow down. Was this what it felt like for the patients she treated? For their families? She was still stuck on one of the first things he'd said to her. Had someone tried to murder her? She was used to life changing in a matter of seconds for other people. One moment she'd been listening to Bach on the radio while driving to the hospital. In the next her vehicle was run off the road and someone was shooting live ammunition—at her.

And then this man—someone who knew her—had saved her life.

Regan wanted to sit up but thought it best to defer to his judgment for the moment. She clenched her lips against the nausea. Concussion for sure—no need for radiation to determine that. All her limbs worked, though slowly, like her electrical impulses were swimming through molasses.

After blinking several times, her fuzzy vision began to clear and the first thing she zeroed in on was an intense set of sapphire-blue eyes. Impossibly dark and captivating. As her view of his face broadened, she took in his well-trimmed beard and brown hair cut short but not messy. More like expertly tousled. How could he look so composed after this encounter when her heart raced like a rabbit that had overdosed on caffeine? He took her hand in both of his to stop her shaking. His broad smile was disarming.

"What happened?" Regan asked. To her, her voice had never sounded so fearful.

Another series of whooping sirens signaled an ambulance struggling to break through the jam of halted vehicles and scared drivers.

"An SUV came up and ran you off the road but…"

Colby's voice trailed. Something definitely troubled him. Regan's chest caved. What could be worse than what had already happened?

"They used a certain maneuver to get your car to spin around like that. You have to be trained in how to do it. Those men who tried to hurt you aren't amateurs."

What did that mean? Regan shook her head. She hadn't had an incident with another driver. Could this just be a case of mistaken identity?

As if reading her mind, Colby said, "This wasn't road rage. I think they wanted to take you."

Kidnap? Regan's body poured more adrenaline into her blood. Could he be right?

"Why do you say that?"

"Because when I picked you up they stopped shooting except for one well-placed round in the hood of my truck. I'm guessing to try and disable it. It seemed like they didn't want to risk hurting you. Did you know those men?"

"I..." Regan tried to process his theory through the cobwebs that spun in her mind. None of this made sense. She was a doctor. A healer. Who could possibly want to hurt her? "I didn't even see them."

Colby raked his hands through his wet hair. "And I didn't have time to get a good look at their license plate."

"How do you know me?" Regan asked.

"My sister is Samantha Waterson." Colby tapped his hefty, black watch. "My family was going to meet with you right about now to discuss whether or not you'd picked her for your research protocol—to save her life."

Regan bit her lip. After all that he had done for her, how could she say no?

"Why do you think they were experts?" Regan asked.

"Because I learned that exact maneuver when I served in the military. What they did wasn't by accident." He nodded behind her, and she eased up and looked behind.

A duo of police officers was walking toward them. He grabbed her hand again, his eyes imploring hers to understand his message. "The police aren't going to find those men and they're going to come back for you. Mark my words."

Regan couldn't connect a logical thought in her mind. Whoever this man was—this stranger, who had saved her life at great risk to his own, seemed to have intuitiveness in understanding the criminal element.

"How do you know they're coming back?"

"I hunt criminals for a living. I know how they act…how they think."

A patrol officer kneeled next to her. "I'm Officer Johnson. I need to ask you a few questions. Your name?"

Regan was still shaky and now the cold was settling into her bones. The rain lightened to a fine mist.

"Regan Lockhart," she answered.

The officer glanced at Colby. "And you are?"

"Colby Waterson."

And in that instant Regan knew she didn't want to be separated from the one man who'd already proved he'd risk his life to protect hers.

TWO

Colby cinched the gray wool blanket the police officer had brought around Regan and then placed his hands on her shoulders to steady her tremors. "You're okay. They're gone. I'm not leaving you."

She looked at him with grateful eyes, and he paused a moment to try to ascertain their exact color. Gray? Green? Right now as dark and brooding as the clouds that had released their payload of rain.

One of the responding officers handed Colby a basic first-aid kit. He popped open the tab and grabbed a package with a large square of gauze, removed it and pressed it gently to her cut. The rain mixed with blood and trickled down her face, making her injury appear more severe than it was. She winced at the pressure and covered his hand with hers in response.

"Sorry," Colby said.

She shook her head. "I don't know what to

say. 'Thank you' seems hardly adequate." Her teeth chattered, and Colby sent a dismayed look to the police officer.

"Any chance we could get her out of the rain?" he asked, his tone edgier than he wanted it to be.

Not only was she trembling from fear but the withdrawal of adrenaline from her system exacerbated her unsteadiness. Add that to the cacophony of voices around her and he was surprised she hadn't shut down completely.

The black GMC had vacated the scene, and Colby gathered from police communications that no one had spotted it. Two paramedics carrying orange trauma packs weaved their way at a jog toward their position.

"Ma'am, can you describe to me what happened?" Officer Johnson asked.

A paramedic kneeled next to her. "Hi, I'm Leonard. What hurts?"

Johnson's partner asked, "Did you get a look at the driver of the other vehicle?"

Colby's chest ached and he could feel his blood just about to boil. He stood and motioned everyone back. "Give her some space," he ordered. "This is what we're going to do." He turned to Johnson. Thunder boomed, and Regan huddled farther into the blanket. "First, out of this rain before it starts to pick back up again. Then, medical gets to take a look at her." He pointed his finger at the officer. "Then a witness statement. Are we clear?"

All nodded, though Johnson narrowed his gaze in a who-does-he-think-he-is glare, but they looked in agreement enough to comply with his demands.

Colby held his hand out to Regan, and she took it willingly but stood too fast. Colby stabilized her with a quick arm around her waist before she fell back down. Regan gripped his arm tightly until her trembling eased. She stood straighter and gave him a gentle smile. Threads of her red hair stuck to the wound on her forehead, and he took his finger and gently eased them away.

He kept his arm around her waist until she was safely sitting in the back of an ambulance, on a gurney. Leonard took the blanket off her shoulders, pushing up Regan's sleeve to take her blood pressure.

"How are you feeling?" he asked.

"Shaky," Regan responded, her voice clearer, in control.

Johnson stepped into the back of the ambulance and Colby traded places with him so he could get close. The officer would be able to get some of the information he needed just from listening to the paramedic's interview.

"Is it all right with you if the officer is here?" Leonard asked.

Regan glanced at her watch. "Whatever speeds this up. I do have patients to see at the hospital. I'm late."

Colby checked the time, as well. Had it been twenty minutes since this thing unfolded? It seemed like just a few had passed. "I'll call the hospital and tell them you're going to be delayed. Be right back."

He stepped down from the rear of the ambulance and walked back to the scene of the crash. Something was going on here—something bad that involved this doctor. His gut was tossing up so many red flags that all he could see was red. The maneuver to push her off the road, in the middle of rush-hour traffic no less, cried of either desperation or determination. Both of which could have proved deadly. He found his cell phone among the shattered glass of his windshield on the floor of his passenger seat and dialed his mother.

"Colby? Are you all right? Where are you?"

Not even a hello. Ever since Sam's cancer, his mother had been a prickly ball of hypersensitive worries, as if at any moment she knew the other shoe was going to drop. Actually, he had himself to blame. His military career had precipitously aged her even before Sam's diagnosis.

Even though his mother was strong in her faith, she seemingly didn't get a dose of the whole "not worrying" thing when God had made her. Maybe worry was an inherited gene as Colby struggled to let God control things, as well.

"I'm fine."

"As in uninjured?" she pressed.

"Yes, not injured, but I've been involved in a little dustup on the highway driving in for Sam's meeting."

"Sam's still in the ICU. These seizures just won't relent. Her doctor's not here yet."

"I know. I'm with her," Colby said.

"With Dr. Lockhart?"

"Yes…it's hard to explain. We were involved in…an accident."

"You hit her? Is she all right? Is she alive?"

The shrill tone of his mother's voice caused him to ease the phone away from his ear. "Mom—"

"Colby, I'd never forgive you. We've been waiting to hear her final decision for weeks."

He got it. He'd never forgive himself if he'd been the one to take away Sam's only hope at living a full life.

"Mom, Sam's doctor is fine, but it's going to be a few hours before we can be at the hospital."

"You're staying with her?" his mother asked, her voice maintaining the same high pitch.

"It's complicated. I'm going to make sure she gets to the hospital okay. Will you tell Sam's nurse, so she can tell whoever else needs to know, that Dr. Lockhart is going to be delayed?"

Colby neared Regan's SUV.

"She can't call herself?"

Colby reached across the driver's seat and found Regan's purse, its contents strewed across the passenger's floor mat. "She doesn't have her phone at the moment. Please, Mom? I need to go."

"All right. Be safe."

Her classic sign-off. It was her habit never to say goodbye. Too much finality, he guessed. She'd once told him she'd only say it if she was sure he was never coming back. Maybe that was what military life did to families. Another reason why she rarely said, "I love you." Even though she did fiercely.

His next call was to his associate, Daniel Green.

"Aren't you at the hospital?"

"I should be. Listen, I need you to bring me your truck. And then stay behind and take care of two vehicles that need to be towed."

"Wow, sounds exactly like how I hoped to be spending my morning. Is this what you meant by 'other jobs as determined by the president' when you hired me?"

"Exactly."

Colby gave him the necessary information and

disconnected the call. Colby's office wasn't far from there. If Dan hurried, it shouldn't take more than fifteen minutes. If he came down the other side of the highway, he wouldn't get stuck in the mass of cars on this side of the road.

Officers were on the highway taking measurements. Orange-and-white-striped cones had been set up, and two traffic cops directed the stream of angry morning commuters to the two lanes on the right side of the road.

Colby brushed the glass off and then sat in Regan's driver's seat. His knees didn't immediately hit his chest like every other car he sat in after a woman had driven it, meaning she was likely just a few inches shorter than he was.

He reached down and began to gather up the items that had spilled from her purse. This was partly to be helpful but also an investigation. Those thugs wanted something from this doctor. Could anything in this car give him a clue as to what that might be?

He reached for her wallet that laid splayed open. The first picture he saw was of a young girl, perhaps ten years old. Her hair the same color as her mother's, but her eyes were blue. He flipped through the photos. No photos with a male presence. He hadn't remembered a wedding ring on the doctor's left hand.

A child meant leverage, and all Colby could

think was that he needed Regan to call her daughter to make sure she was okay.

He grabbed her black purse, snapped the wallet closed and put it inside. Under the passenger seat, he found her phone. When his thumb brushed the screen it displayed her most recent messages. Nothing questionable that would explain this predicament. He threw that in the purse, as well.

After that, he snagged the few items scattered about that were foreign to his hands ever since his wife had died from the same cursed disease that now ravaged his sister. A tube of lipstick. A compact with mirror. A nail file.

He brushed his finger against the fine sandpaper and thought about how chemo had taken away from his wife even the little things she'd enjoyed—like doing her nails. They'd become so brittle, her fingers numb from the chemo, that she hadn't liked them to be touched. Her death had been his entry ticket into the military. It was easier to run away than face a lonely life without her.

Colby clutched the purse in his hand, stepped away from the SUV and then opened up the back passenger-side door. The seat was littered with several medical journals that had likely been tucked in a neat pile. He stood in the empty traffic lane and glanced up the highway, a smattering of cars ahead of him.

What did these events mean? Was Regan truly in danger? And if she was, what did that mean for Sam?

The tension in Regan's chest eased when Colby stepped up into the back of the ambulance, her purse clutched in one of his hands. Her shaking had stopped and the chill was replaced with warmth from his gentle inquisitive smile.

"Everything okay?" he asked, his eyes only engaging hers.

"I keep telling the officer that I really didn't see anything."

"What about you, sir?" The officer turned in his direction. "What did you see?"

"I'll tell you briefly what I know, but is there any reason to delay her medical care?"

The officer raised his chin at Colby in defiance to his testiness. "Aren't you a bounty hunter?"

"Fugitive recovery officer."

"Same thing, right?"

"We just prefer not to be called bounty hunters."

Regan rustled through her purse and found her phone, pulling up a quick screen to text her daughter, Olivia.

Colby nudged the officer to one side. “Are you checking on your daughter?”

Regan’s finger froze against the cool surface of her phone screen. “How did you know I had a daughter?” she asked, her voice slightly off-kilter. What did she know about this man, really? Could he be involved with the people who had run her off the road? Simply offering her assistance as a ruse to gain her trust?

“I saw her picture in your wallet.”

“You looked through it?” Regan asked, wondering what he might have seen that she didn’t want him to.

“No. It had popped open. Everything spilled out of your purse, but I will say I didn’t find any clues.”

“Clues for what?”

“For why those men might have been after you.”

The officer turned Colby’s way. “So you don’t think this was an accident?”

“Not in the least. They used a specific maneuver to get her off the road. The only person they seemed to be shooting at was me. As soon as I picked her up to get her to a safer place, they fired less directly. They wore ski masks to cover their faces. I didn’t get a look at their license plate.”

“There are thousands of those black GMCs

in the city." The officer zeroed in on Regan. "Ma'am, do you have any idea why these men would be after you?"

Something broke inside Regan's mind at that point. It was all becoming too much to comprehend. The accident. A handsome stranger saving her and continuing to provide assistance. It was the stuff of fairy tales and couldn't be part of her trajectory, which was either men hurting her or them being professionally threatened by her success. Regan led the most boring life of anyone she knew outside of her groundbreaking research. Her life consisted of going to the hospital, seeing patients, going home and trying to give Olivia the last shreds of her energy. She'd never been involved in anything illegal—ever.

Unless…

Her phone pinged in her hand, causing her to jump and her thoughts to scatter. "My daughter's okay," she said to no one in particular.

"Good," both the officer and Colby said.

Regan couldn't help but roll her eyes. It was a contest of the most concerned male in the back of the ambulance. "Listen, I don't know why these men would have been after me. If I had to guess, I'd say they had the wrong person. Is there anything else all of you need?"

The officer shook his head. "We just need to get your SUV towed off the road."

"I've taken care of that," Colby said.

"I'll file an accident report," the officer responded. "This case will be reviewed by a detective to see if assault with a deadly weapon charges should be filed, as well."

Regan sat up. "That's if you can even find these creeps, right?"

"We'll take you to the hospital," Leonard said.

Regan stood. Her vision blurred and she reached out blindly to hold on to something to steady herself when she felt Colby's arm around her shoulders. She was surprised at how she liked the strength he offered.

"Steady now," he cautioned.

"I'm not paying for an ambulance ride to get some stitches." Regan opened her eyes and found Colby's blue eyes searching hers.

"We're both going to the same place. I'll give you a ride," Colby said.

"In your truck? The one that no longer has a windshield?"

"An associate of mine is bringing another vehicle."

"Great." She turned to the paramedic. "Looks like I've got a cheaper invitation."

Even when she thought she should have hesitated, she didn't. Given the slim chance Colby could be part of what happened, the police had his identifying information and he'd put himself in harm's way for her. Likely the only reason he wanted to help was to ensure she stayed alive long enough to perform his sister's operation.

The police officer handed her his card. "In case you think of anything. I'll call you later today to update you."

She plucked the card from his fingertips. "Great."

Colby jumped from the back of the ambulance and reached his hand up to her.

The rain had stopped and she could see the sun trying to break through the gray in the distance. Colby waved to a man on the other side of the highway who stood near a white truck the same make and model as Colby's.

"I forgot one thing." He raced a few steps ahead of her and scrounged around in his car until he came up with a set of dog tags. "Now, we need to get to the other side of the road."

Colby helped her climb over the cement median and waited for a lull in traffic before he pulled her, running, across the highway. Her pounding footsteps only intensified her headache.

Colby and the other man exchanged a few words before the man crossed the highway toward the ruined wreckage that remained of their vehicles. Regan climbed into the white truck and slid over to the passenger seat. Colby hung the dog tags from the rearview mirror.

She clipped the seat belt and fingered the metal rectangles. “A friend?”

Colby nodded and pressed his lips together, moving the truck into the river of cars.

“You were in the military?”

He glanced her way. A sad smile mirrored the grief in his eyes.

Regan hugged her purse. It really was the curse of every medical professional. It was her job to sit and ask those questions that no one else would ask—intimate details of a person’s life laid out in front of her so she could make the best medical decision. Sometimes it was just hard to know when to dial it back.

As if to cut her some slack, he answered her question. “Delta Force.”

“Are those tags from a friend of yours?”

“Mark. An old friend. I can’t risk losing them at some body shop when my truck gets fixed.” Pain etched his words.

“How many years did you serve?”

“Too many. Not enough.”

Great. Just what she needed. The strong, silent type. Of course, her ex-husband had been a violent, verbally abusive monster, so perhaps this was a move in the right direction.

What am I thinking? He’s dealing with a sister

who has cancer. I'm a single mom. I have enough on my plate. He has enough on his. Lord, help me to focus on the right things here.

"Why did you leave the military?" Regan asked.

"Sam."

His eyes glistened as he turned away from her, and her throat thickened at his quick emotional response. Clinically, she knew a lot about Samantha Waterson. Age twenty-eight. Grade four glioblastoma—the worst kind of brain tumor, resistant to surgery and aggressive chemotherapy. These patients sought Regan out when conventional medicine failed to destroy the malicious cells that replaced healthy tissue with dysfunctional ones.

Interacting with Colby personalized his sister to her in a way that was sometimes hard as a doctor to cross over—seeing the person instead of just the brain MRI.

"Had you decided whether or not you were going to take Sam's case?" he asked without taking his eyes off the road.

"I never set up a face-to-face meeting until I know the patient is a candidate. A strong candidate. I actually have her on the surgery schedule for tomorrow morning."

That was true. Regan had developed the policy after meeting with too many patients who weren't an appropriate fit for the study. She'd pray, relentlessly, for help in making the right decision. Was giving false hope better than dealing with death? Regan wasn't strong enough to decline treatment when families sobbed in front of her. What human could? It was the part of medicine she hated—her inability to defeat death.

"Good." Colby nodded and wiped away a quick tear, sniffing hard as if to urge the other potential droplets of his fear to stay in their place. "I guess my one and only job is to get you to the hospital safely. Get you all fixed up and then on to save Sam's life."

His statement was like a knife to her heart. There was so much expectation in those few words and she didn't want to disappoint him.

Because, like Colby, she wasn't sure she'd seen the last of those men. Could he be a man she could trust if they came back?

She glanced back at her SUV as they merged into traffic—the passenger side completely mashed up against the concrete and all of the windows shattered. Now that most of her adrenaline had dissipated, she was becoming cognizant of the mild aches and pains that would bloom into full-body soreness and immobility in the next few days, and she didn't know if she'd feel safe operating on someone's brain tomorrow.

Her cure couldn't work if the patient died on the operating room table.

THREE

Olivia wasn't answering her texts.

It was nearly midnight before Regan left the hospital. First the car accident. Could it be called that? Was potential vehicular homicide a more accurate term? Followed by stitches in the ER and then patient appointments the rest of the day. Above all else, she didn't want her personal circumstances to affect the care of her patients. So many patients were desperate to participate in her research protocol, which showed true promise in curing the most aggressive type of brain tumor.

And she was using a polio virus to do it.

The cost of that decision was getting home way past Olivia's bedtime, and the last thing she needed was to worry about her eleven-year-old daughter and the growing distance between them.

Sadly, medicine taught doctors to assume the worst-case scenario first and then settle on the more realistic diagnosis once the life-threatening possibilities were ruled out. Simply, an unanswered text first meant someone had died—plain and simple. Or they were stranded in a ditch and near death. No other possibility was acceptable until that one was ruled out.

Adding to this certainty was that her nanny, Polina, didn't answer her texts or phone calls, either.

Lord, just let them be safe.

Regan fingered the front of her phone to call up the screen and smoothed her thumb over the picture of Olivia. Regan hadn't thought eleven would be a hard age to deal with, but it was turning into exactly that. Her usually joyful and optimistic child had turned surly and ambivalent. Were the hormones changing more than her body? Or was it something more, something that Regan couldn't change, like being away from home so much? The clinical trial consumed nearly every extra moment she could spare. Scraps of her attention. That was what Olivia got. She wanted to change this, but also needed to provide for Olivia—for all that she thought she deserved.

Why hadn't Olivia called? Regan's routine with Olivia when she was at the hospital was to talk every night if she didn't make it home by dinner. If Regan couldn't take the time to chat, she would send a quick text. But her call went to voice mail—her text with a multitude of heart and flower emojis unanswered, like silent witnesses to the distance between them.

Regan tapped her fingers on the front of her phone, trying to disperse the anxious tingling of her fingertips. She was breathing too fast. It was making her headache come back in full force.

Slow it down, Regan, slow it down. Stop thinking like this.

It wasn't the first time an evening call went unanswered—but it was rare.

As the garage door rose, Polina's battered navy blue Chevy Cavalier was where it should be. Regan parked her rental car, grabbed her purse and exited the vehicle, but froze when she saw the door that led into her kitchen. It stood open—all the way. The interior of the house was as dark and deep as a water well. The garage light flickered off and Regan's heartbeat raced as blackness and fear enveloped her.

It was quiet—too quiet.

"Olivia? Polina?"

A stillness like no human presence remained. Regan pulled out her phone and activated the flashlight, approaching the wooden steps that led into the house with measured caution. Her heart galloped in her chest.

As the light traveled up the door frame, a

smudge of blood jumped out in deep contrast to the white. When Regan crested the top step, heavy black marks and chipped paint gave the door a distressed look that had not been present before. As Regan entered the mudroom and eased the door closed behind her, she nearly tripped on bottles of laundry supplies that sat scattered on the marble tile. The box of laundry detergent had turned over and spilled. Soapy white crystals spread out like a blizzard had raced through the room. On the backside of the door, dusty footprints marred the white paint in several areas, almost as if someone had planted feet there to prevent the door from being opened. They were too large to be Olivia's. The tread marks seemed characteristic of the athletic shoes Polina often wore.

Regan stepped farther into the house, throwing on every light switch as she briskly walked by, flooding the darkness to keep her evil thoughts at bay. The desk in her kitchen had been ransacked. Her papers, bills and notes were scattered all across the floor. A few more steps and she crossed broken glass from strewed dinner dishes. She wasn't sure at first glance if the red liquid splashed against her refrigerator was spaghetti sauce or blood.

Rushing up the tan-carpeted stairs, Regan headed straight into Olivia's room.

And there was the bed, perfectly made.

"Olivia!" she screamed, her sobs the only answer.

She rushed across to hall to Polina's room and was met by another neatly made bed. Regan crossed to the center of the room, looking for any clue that would explain their disappearances, her briefcase still clutched in her hand, her breath strangled by invisible pythons wrapping and tightening themselves around her chest.

Regan's phone pinged—an incoming text. Her vision blurred from the onslaught of tears. She brought her phone to her face.

Whatever you do—don't call the police. Go downstairs. You'll find what you're looking for.

Regan's hands shook and she tumbled to her knees. Whoever had Olivia was watching her. Had they followed her home? Were there cameras? Or were they merely watching her shadow travel through the windows to determine her position in the house? Did they sickly observe and relish the fact that her life was changing forever? Were they here? Inside her home? She didn't want to go downstairs. Had she missed them? Were Olivia and Polina's bodies lying somewhere downstairs and she had run past them, hoping to find them sleeping peacefully in their beds?

Terror crystallized every functioning cell in a wintry ice Regan didn't believe she'd ever be free from. Should she call 9-1-1? Was the text instructing her not to because the assailants were waiting downstairs? Her heartbeat echoed in her ears like a scream in a canyon. Who could she reach out to? Her career caused isolation. Her parents believed her ex-husband's stories that Regan's study of medicine had caused the demise of her marriage, and so they didn't stay in touch, not even for Olivia's sake. Sadly, Regan didn't know much about Polina's family, or if they could help her grope through this shock to find help.

Regan took several deep breaths to abate the tremor stealing the strength from her legs. She stood, shaky, and took the stairs back down, leaning heavily against the banister to stay upright.

As her feet hit the landing, she almost dropped to her knees again—the terror quickly leaching the strength from her muscles. Retracing her steps, she entered the kitchen, seemingly Olivia and Polina's last stand, and found a card lying on her granite island—the bawdy fluorescent green almost mocking.

It was Olivia's handwriting on the back of the envelope. *Mommy.*

Regan crumpled against the counter, pulling the envelope toward her. She slid her blood-drained finger under the envelope's flap, ripped through the paper and removed the card.

A ransom note.

We have your daughter. In order to get her back alive, we need you to do the following...

Colby stood on the sidewalk in front of Regan Lockhart's home. A mix of emotions hazed his thoughts. One, he was angry she hadn't showed up for Sam's surgery this morning. Two, he was disappointed because he had been looking forward to seeing her again. But, overwhelmingly, he was worried. Did the events of yesterday have anything to do with today? Had they been a precursor to a bigger event? A crime even?

In hunting fugitives, starting at home base was often the first step. Then Colby would check friends and criminal cohorts. There was always a place to start.

Time to find out what the doctor was hiding.

It hadn't taken long to find Regan's house. It was not as he'd expected it to be...a smallish, refurbished Craftsman home, not five minutes from the hospital. Nothing looked out of the ordinary. Above all else, she had to open the door—even if it took a ruse to do it. He jogged up the steps and pounded three times on the black door.

"Dr. Lockhart!"

Colby quickly stepped back from the door. His plan was to put his foot in the crack as soon as she opened it, and if she didn't quickly agree to return to the hospital, he was going to throw her over his shoulder and carry her there himself.

But as soon as the door opened and he began to advance, two metallic barbed instruments of torture hit Colby square in the chest and every muscle in his body contracted.

A Taser.

It felt like he'd just hit his funny bone, the feeling multiplying with lightning speed through every nerve in his body. He fell straight forward onto his face, his nose punching into the cement and blood popping from broken blood vessels. He inhaled the coppery-tasting fluid down the back of his throat as he struggled to open his mouth to breathe. Closing his eyes against the vertigo seemed like his only option.

"Mr. Waterson! What are you doing here?"

He felt Regan's hands at his shoulder and waist as she pulled him over to his back, quickly plucking the darts from his chest. She was stronger than he'd imagined.

Did she really have to ask, considering the plight she had left Sam in? Colby tried to answer but the dizziness, even with his eyes closed, had him about to toss his breakfast onto Regan's lap.

She laid a calming hand on his chest. "I'm sorry. It's just that you scared me. Why didn't you just tell me it was you?"

What could he say? *I'm so mad about Sam's surgery being canceled that I want you arrested and held until you can do said operation. I didn't know if you'd even remember me. If you'd still trust me enough, considering what happened yesterday, to open the door.*

"Can you sit up?"

Colby held up a hand to stop her, still afraid if he opened his mouth he couldn't control what might happen next—both by his body or his language. Worsening his nausea was the blood he was swallowing. He looked up, focusing on the sky and the gray fall clouds brewing black with another threat of rain. Breathing slowly, he felt the dizziness abate and he placed his hands behind him and pushed up. Blood from his nose began to drip onto his shirt.

Regan reached forward and pinched his nostrils together. He winced from the pain, though it was markedly less than the full-body muscle soreness he now suffered, akin to lifting weights in the gym for twelve hours. It surprised him that she didn't hold anything as a barrier from his blood when it was likely ingrained in her DNA to never do such a thing. That could mean she was willing to risk her life to do whatever needed to be done. Perhaps it was the same thing that made her a medical research maverick.

Never in his life had a woman surprised him like that. It was the last thing he'd expected from the lithe, uber-intellectual doctor. There was a definite fire within her.

After countless minutes, she released her fingers but kept a palm open underneath his nose to catch any stray droplets.

"Why are you here?" Colby asked, the words more angry than he intended. As he'd feared, she backed away from him, her trepidation filling the space. She was afraid of something. He softened his voice. "Why didn't you come to the hospital for Sam's surgery? Are you all right?"

Regan sat back on her heels and looked away from him, her hands clasped tightly in her lap.

What could he expect from her? Why should she trust him?

He folded shaky arms around his legs, not sure he could stand without falling. "Whatever it is, I want to help. Not just for Sam but..."

For you, too? Was that what he was going to say? Was it more than desperation for Sam tugging at his heartstrings?

Regan gripped her thighs, her hands white with blue fingertips from the frigid breeze that blew and pulled dead leaves from skeleton branches.

Colby took a deep breath and the sharp, crisp air set his lungs on fire.

Silent tears fell down her face. What would cause a woman, who seemingly had dedicated her life to healing, to abandon a patient and her clinical trial? He'd asked himself this question over and over again because only when he knew the answer could he save her.

And save Sam.

"I'm here to help you so that you can still help Sam. If something happens to you, no one else will be able to do the surgery—or have the cure."

Regan's lips trembled and she pressed the back of her pale hand against her lips. Her silence wasn't defiance at his request…it was fear.

Colby eased up to his knees and reached for the hand hanging limp at her side. He held it and rubbed the back of it with his thumb, hoping the friction would ease the chill. "Please…I can and will help you. Whatever it is. I'll do anything to save Sam's life."

Her gray-green eyes took him in, measuring him with an intensity that caused his heart to skip several beats. Few women caused such a rise.

"Someone has taken my daughter, Olivia. As ransom, they want the modified polio virus. Your sister's cure." She raised an eyebrow…almost as a challenge to his resolve.

He stood, using her porch railing for support, and reached a hand out to her. “I think we need to go inside and talk. What you don’t know about mc is that I’m used to finding bad guys…and it seems like some bad guys have your daughter.”

At first she wouldn’t do it—take his hand. He’d seen the look in women before who’d had less than ideal relationships with men, and he felt like he was asking the rabbit to trust the wolf. But then, ever so slowly, she reached out for him and took his hand. With his other hand, he clenched her elbow and pulled her up.

And in that moment, their eyes meeting, Colby wondered if he was trading his life for Sam’s.

FOUR

Regan trembled. It had been years since she'd had a man in her home. Colby's inquisitive stare took in what remained of the home invasion that had snatched Olivia and Polina from what Regan considered a very safe house.

"When did you discover that they were missing?" Colby asked. He sat on her white couch, leaned forward and settled his elbows on his knees, his muscles still quivering from the effects of the Taser.

Hurting Colby added to the weight in her gut—so many misdeeds she needed to confess. What would he do when he found out what she'd done? Would he still help her?

"Last night when I got home. The house was a disaster—evidence of a struggle here on the lower level. When I was upstairs searching for Olivia and Polina, I got a text that told me to go back to the kitchen."

"What did the text say?"

"It instructed me not to call law enforcement. To go back downstairs—which is where the ransom note was."

"So they were watching you."

Regan nodded. "I think so but from outside. I've searched the house pretty intently and didn't find anything I would consider a camera or listening device."

Colby glanced around. "Not exactly your area of expertise, either. Is the house unattended for long periods of time?"

Regan shook her head. "Polina is almost always here."

"My guess is they had someone trailing you, but I couldn't guarantee it was just that."

The strength leached from her legs, and Regan sat next to Colby. Both stared straight ahead. Regan's heart thundered in her chest. She needed to tell him before he made a commitment he wouldn't back away from. At least, that was the kind of man she read Colby to be. Someone who wouldn't walk away from a fight once he'd agreed to step into the ring.

"Let me see the note."

Regan's voice tightened. "I need to tell you something first."

She stood without glancing back at him, walked to the front closet and pulled out the cooler she'd tucked into the corner under her full-length coats.

"What's in there?" His voice was already full of suspicion.

"The modified polio virus. Your sister's cure."

"All of it?" he asked.

She nodded. "Yes, all of it. Those were the instructions. We only manufacture enough for a few patients at a time. I stole it from the hospital early this morning. This is what the kidnappers want for Olivia's life. This is what the ransom note is asking me to exchange her for."

Colby leaned back into the sofa, somewhat deflated. "So you're not going to give them an alternative—something they believe could be the virus."

"I won't do anything that will risk Olivia's life."

Colby raised his hands in disbelief. "But you're risking everyone else's life—*everyone* who is hoping that their lives could be saved by what's in those vials."

"She's my daughter," Regan cried. "I'm hoping I can somehow get Olivia back without giving up my life's work—and so many people's hope at a full life."

"What was your plan, exactly?"

She shrugged and took a seat opposite him in a gray chair, holding the cooler on her lap.

The look on his face—contemplative. For several minutes he looked everywhere but at her. Was he considering dropping his offer? What would she do then?

"Do you understand how serious this is?" he finally asked her.

"Of course—"

"Not just for Olivia and your nanny, but for you, as well. For your professional career?"

The ends of her fingers tingled and she gripped the cooler tighter. "What do you expect me to do? Give it back before Olivia's safe?"

"Regan, did the hospital give you permission to take what's in that cooler?"

He was driving straight at the matter—with a red-hot poker. She shook her head.

"You've stolen hospital property. You've abandoned your patients. Your professional livelihood is at risk—I'd say holding on by a thread at this point."

Her throat ached and she swallowed heavily. Of course, he was right. But what would her life be worth if her daughter was dead? Losing her medical license was the least of her concerns.

"Will you still help me? Or are you going to turn me in?"

Colby straightened and leaned toward her. "You're trying to save Olivia. I'm trying to save

Sam. But helping you may not accomplish my goal. The cure may be lost."

There it was. Men had a bottom line that seemed to always align against her interests. Of course, it had been too much to hope for. A knight in shining armor. Someone she could trust to help her sort through this mess. What was he trying to do, exactly? Force her to do something she wasn't willing to do—give him the one thing that would save Olivia? What would he do—take the cooler from her and return it to the hospital?

One thing she'd stopped doing a long time ago was begging a man to help her solve her problems. If he volunteered—great, but she wasn't going to grovel. She had done enough of that toward the end of her marriage and all she'd gotten was an ex-husband who'd abandoned his daughter and two sets of grandparents who wouldn't give her the time of day.

"I'm not giving this to you to give back to the hospital. So, if you've decided not to help me then you need to leave."

Colby captured her eyes with his, a prison of blue that was somehow comforting. "Show me the ransom note. I need to know exactly what it says."

Regan's fingers trembled as she pulled the card from the envelope and handed it to him. It was simple in its request. The cure for Olivia. The exchange to happen in relatively wooded area at a park nearby.

Colby placed the note back in the envelope. "Why do you think they want this so badly? I mean, enough to take your daughter? It's a very extreme measure. Why not just break into the hospital and grab it? Or pay someone at your lab a nice sum of money to merely give them a sample. Isn't it fairly easy to replicate?"

"Not as easy as you might think."

"I think the more important question is who wants it. Do you have any idea?" Colby asked.

"Desperate people will do desperate things."

"Of course, but what does that mean in this context?"

"Could be other patients. Parents of patients. I haven't considered this treatment yet for pediatric patients but I've been getting inundated with requests from parents to try it on their children."

Colby shook his head. "This is beyond a group of desperate parents. There's nothing else you can think of?"

She paused a little too long before saying, "I'm in the dark as much as you are."

There was something there he couldn't quite put his finger on. Deception took all kinds of forms. Bald-faced lying was one of them and her statement didn't rise to that level. However, denial was just as powerful, and he wondered if there was something in her past she didn't recognize as a threat or didn't want to confess to him as a possible scenario.

Trust. She didn't trust him enough—not yet.

"How did they get into the house?"

"When I came home, the door to the garage was definitely beat up."

"Show me."

He followed her slim frame through the kitchen to the laundry room. Definitely seemed like a last stand had taken place in the small room. Though somewhat picked up, soap crystals crushed under his boots as he examined the door. It was marred as she said—as if someone had put their weight against the door, through whatever means necessary, to keep it from opening. He grabbed a T-shirt from the laundry basket and opened the door. The doorjamb appeared untouched. Not pried open.

"Does your nanny leave the garage door open?"

"Her name's Polina. And of course not."

When he crossed the threshold into her home, the front door seemed untouched, as well. "Are there any broken windows? Other doors that lead into your home?"

"No broken windows. There's only one other door that leads inside from the backyard."

He followed her there, as well. Same story. Different door. The intruders hadn't pried their way in.

"What are you thinking?" she asked.

"If it's not Polina's habit to keep the garage door open, then I would imagine she keeps the door leading from the garage unlocked. Most people do. Which means they opened the garage door to gain entry into the house."

"How would they do that?"

"There are devices that can mimic a garage door signal. They're not that hard to find..." His voice dropped. This whole scenario of hers didn't add up. A group of desperate family members coming together to kidnap a child for a cure. Wouldn't they also need the hand that delivered it? "Take me through the rest of the house."

The main level left convincing evidence of a home invasion. He took in the desk—the drawers opened with such force that the wood had fractured. File folders open on the desk. Some with knife slits through the middle.

"Did you keep any information about the virus here?"

"No. Only at the lab and..."

"And?" Colby pressured.

"It's not important to what's happened here."

Colby let the comment slide but her refusal to expand added to his level of belief that she wasn't fully disclosing her thoughts on what had happened.

"Anything upstairs?"

"It looked undisturbed."

"Let's have a look, anyway. Now that you've passed the initial shock you might see something that you hadn't noticed before."

Upstairs, they stood in the middle of Olivia's room, seemingly undisturbed.

"Do you notice anything?" Regan asked.

Colby couldn't push the thought from his head. If they were prepared to hold Olivia for ransom, and they were professionals, wouldn't they plan for some contingencies? Unless they thought Regan would capitulate immediately and she'd have her daughter back tomorrow night. Two days to accomplish what they'd ask for. But what if she hadn't?

"Look through her clothes. Do you see anything missing?"

Regan opened Olivia's closet and first peered up. "Her suitcase is missing."

Colby motioned to her dresser. "How much clothing?"

She stepped over to the dresser and paused, her fingers clutched on the knobs of the top drawer. "What does it mean if her clothes are gone?"

"It would probably be a good sign. That they

were wanting to provide for her needs and not just wanting to…"

Regan nodded. Colby didn't need to speak out loud what both of them knew. She pulled the top drawer open, snapped it closed, and then yanked open the other drawers. After pushing them all closed, she turned around and fell against the dresser, her hands covering her eyes.

Colby didn't know the right response. Women crying always befuddled him and the two of them had been thrust together into a situation that required emotional comfort but needed logistical thought. They had to be strong. To think first. Plan.

But something within him, something that had been missing since his wife's death, stirred briefly and he raised his hand to place it on her shoulder.

She dropped her hands and so did he before he made a gesture that might be misinterpreted.

"Many of her clothes are missing."

Colby peered at the bottom of the closet. There was an empty basket. He didn't see another clothes hamper. That meant the empty drawers would be a good indication of how much they'd taken.

"What's left of her clothes? Are they still folded on the inside?" Colby asked.

"Yes, why?"

"It makes me think Polina packed the suitcase, then, and not the intruders just riffling through in a hurry to grab a few things to tide them over."

"Then Polina should have clothes missing, as well?"

"Let's check."

Before leaving Olivia's room, Colby peered out her window, which gave a front view of the street. The roads were empty. No signs of a vehicle he would consider suspicious for surveillance. Then again, why would they need to watch Regan when they controlled her by having the one thing she considered most precious?

Inside Polina's room a different story had been written. Her suitcase remained in the closet. Her drawers appeared full. A small amount of clothing was in the laundry basket at the bottom of the bed.

"What do you think it means?" Regan asked.

Even though they both knew.

Things didn't look good for Polina's survivability.

"Let's go back downstairs. Look at the note again. Develop our game plan."

Once downstairs, Colby grabbed the note and sat on the couch. Regan sat next to him, peering over his shoulder as he examined the contents. Her closeness made it difficult to concentrate and he scooted a few inches away from her.

“First thing, we can’t operate out of your house. Once the hospital discovers the virus is gone, the cops are going to be on your tail.”

“It will probably be more than the local police,” Regan said.

Colby turned to Regan. “Meaning?”

“I think the hospital would potentially report it to Homeland Security.”

“It’s not a lethal virus. Right?”

“Right. But that doesn’t mean…”

“Mean what? It’s like there’s something you don’t want to say. Whatever you’re thinking, you need to say it. Keeping something hidden from me won’t help us solve this.”

“Viruses can always potentially be manipulated into something more virulent. Or, at least, someone could try.”

Colby’s chest tightened. That had to be it. Definitely a more plausible explanation than her rogue desperate parent theory. There was more there. He was sure of it. But for now, if that was all she was willing to disclose, he’d go with it.

What it meant? That their enemy could be that much more nefarious.

“We need to find a hotel somewhere close to this park. Scope it out tonight before the drop-off tomorrow.”

“I need to exchange these vials for something completely benign. I need to protect what’s here.”

"So you never intended to give it to them? Why take it?"

"Don't you think it was wise to make them believe I was somewhat complying with their plan?"

"Probably."

"However, if it comes down to Olivia's life, I can't say I won't choose that path."

Tears flowed down her cheeks, and this time he couldn't help himself. He reached up and thumbed them off her face. Heat raced up his arm from that one touch. "Let's not think worst-case scenario. Not yet. We need to keep our heads in the game." Did he say that for her benefit?

Or more for his own?

"I know someone with a private lab who wouldn't ask too many questions if I asked him to store it. He could at least give me something that resembled what's in the cooler."

"Vial wise or biologically, as well?"

"Both."

She picked up her cell phone. Colby snatched it from her hand. "You can't use this." He powered it down. "And I probably shouldn't use mine."

"How would they know you're helping me?"

"It's not going to be a reach. I stormed out of the hospital saying I was going to look for you. We need to assume the authorities know we're together—and that mind-set will hopefully prevent us from leaving clues behind. Do you have cash on hand?"

"Not much. A couple hundred dollars at most."

At least Colby planned for such contingencies such as needing to be on the run or at least off grid for a period of time. "Don't worry. I've got some additional resources we can tap into."

A car door slammed. Both of them sat up straighter.

"Are you expecting someone?" Colby asked.

Regan shook her head.

Colby motioned her down onto the floor. He then army-crawled to the front window, lifted the lower edge of the curtain and peered out.

A nondescript black SUV. One man stood by it—dressed in tactical gear.

Not good.

He turned back to Regan. "We need to go, now." His voice was low but with as much urgency as he could muster without yelling at her.

She scrambled toward the cooler and picked it up, grabbing her purse that sat next to it.

"Back door?" he whispered.

She motioned to the back of the house. They crawled to the door together. He looked through the window. Didn't see anyone…not yet, at least. There was a wooded lot just beyond her property. That was where he'd hidden his motorcycle. Probably not the best mode of transportation but easy to conceal, which was why he'd chosen it—not imagining he'd be pulling Regan behind him for an escape. He merely hadn't wanted her to see him coming.

"We need to run for those trees as fast as we can."

He saw Regan glance down at her shoes. Modest high heels, but high heels nonetheless. He thought about asking her to take them off but she was likely comfortable in them and she'd need the barrier to keep her running across rocks and sticks. "You'll be fine. Just keep your head low."

He motioned her to the side, unlocked the dead bolt and opened the door an inch. Nothing happened, which hopefully meant they'd beaten them to the back door.

The doorbell rang, followed by three successive knocks. "Dr. Lockhart! I'm with the military! We have a few questions for you!"

Colby grabbed her arm. "On three."

FIVE

Before Colby could begin to count, Regan heard the tinkling of breaking glass followed by an eardrum-rupturing explosion. Abandoning the count, Colby pushed her forward, and Regan lost her footing, tumbling forward and losing her grip on the cooler. He snatched it up and grabbed her hand, pulling her to a standing position.

"Run!"

They ran pell-mell into the tree line, Colby holding the cooler with one hand and Regan's hand with the other. She gripped her purse against her shoulder with her other arm. He wove through the trees like an expert off-trail skier, pulling her behind him. A canister landed in front of them, Colby immediately picked it up and chucked it to the side. It began to smoke in the distance.

Tear gas.

Bullets tore through branches and leaves

rained down on their heads. Colby pulled her down into the underbrush, dirt flying into her face as he positioned himself prone and looked into the wake from where they had come.

Two men were stalking them, walking forward slowly. They were off to the right and the direction they were heading had them in a trajectory that wouldn't intercept where they were hiding. However, if they moved, they would certainly alert them to their presence. Colby fingered through the dead leaves and produced a fragmented bit of black plastic.

"Rubber bullets," he whispered.

Regan nodded. From her years of physician training, she knew rubber bullets were less lethal but could still produce significant injury if the victim was hit the right way. However, the tear gas and use of less lethal ammunitions meant these men were more interested in detaining them than in killing them.

Regan reached for the cooler and pulled it close to her body. The two men continued to veer right, in the direction of the spent tear gas canister, when another man broached the tree line.

Colby inhaled sharply, his hand tightening around hers. "I know that guy."

They both remained prone, covered well by a grouping of waist-high bushes. "From where?" Regan whispered.

"The military. Delta Force. We served together."

"Maybe we should just surrender then," Regan said.

Colby shook his head. "Never surrender until you know the intention of your enemy."

Why had Colby called a man he'd served with the enemy? Particularly former comrades.

A car engine roared to life as someone pressed on the accelerator with the car in Neutral. Regan reflexively rolled her eyes. There was a gentleman who lived on the street behind her who repaired cars out of his garage. This daily occurrence was usually annoying, but now Regan might need to bake him cookies because it drew all three men off in a run away from them.

Colby patted her back and motioned in the other direction. They hustled, half bent over, Colby taking the lead. After several minutes they came to a small clearing in the trees where Regan spied what was non-affectionately known as a death machine in medicine.

A motorcycle.

Regan pulled away from Colby. Even if their lives were in danger, she couldn't imagine getting on the back. It was black with burnt orange metallic accents. New or at the very least idolized. He took her purse and the cooler from her hands and set them on the ground. Taking off his black leather jacket, he handed it to her and then muscled her purse into a small saddlebag. Without instruction, she put it on, swallowed up by the heavy fabric and the scent of his cologne. Colby grabbed the black helmet from the seat and handed it to her. She held it in her hand like a foreign object.

"Put it on," he ordered.

It seemed ridiculous to argue and Regan tried to push from her mind the hundreds of surgeries she'd performed on brain-injured patients from crashing on these bikes.

"Where's yours?"

"That is mine. I didn't think I'd be taking you with me." He straddled the bike and pulled it upright. "Regan, hurry. Pick the cooler up. It's not going to take them long to figure out they went the wrong direction."

She handed him the cooler and pushed the helmet over her head. Definitely too big, but it would afford some protection if she fell off or they crashed. Colby motioned her forward and tightened the strap under her chin, which only mildly improved the situation. He grabbed her arm and helped her up. The passenger seat, if that was even the correct term, was perched higher than Colby's seat and it forced her forward, the front of her body against his back.

Colby kept the cooler pinned between him and the front of the bike. "You're going to need to reach around me and hold the cooler in place so I can drive." He clasped her hands and pulled her forward so she was snuggled tightly against his back. Her fingers felt the cool plastic handle and she gripped it tightly.

The motorcycle roared to life when suddenly something sharp hit Regan square in her mid-back. She gasped, released the cooler from her hands and began to fall off the bike to the left. Colby turned and grabbed her before her body was introduced to the ground. Regan patted her lower back and brought her hand up. No blood.

As Colby steadied her, his eyes narrowed, and Regan turned to see what he'd zeroed in on. Regan glanced back.

They'd been found.

Regan resituated herself on the bike, thrust her arms forward, found the cooler again and held it tightly. "Go!"

The motorcycle surged forward, Colby taking a deep right turn, kicking up dirt and grass. Regan closed her eyes, her stomach in her throat. The vibration of the engine tingled every nerve in her body.

"Don't let go!" Colby ordered.

One thing she knew—if she let go of Colby in that moment, she would die.

* * *

Colby turned into the parking lot of a run-down highway motel and stopped the engine. He held the bike centered, allowing Regan to climb down before he set the kickstand in place. He couldn't help but smile as Regan walked, legs slightly wider, to shake off the muscle tiredness of sitting on a bike for over an hour. She pulled the helmet off her head, her red hair spilling onto her slender shoulders.

She turned back to him with a smile on her face and a mischievous gleam in her eyes. "I might have to change my mind about these things."

"Fun, right?"

However the smile melted from her face as soon as she closed the distance between them, her hand reaching behind her.

"Take off the jacket. Let me look," Colby said.

Regan eased the jacket off her shoulders and handed it to him. Colby pushed himself off the bike, set the cooler on the ground and laid the jacket over the bike seat. He walked around so she wouldn't have to move anymore.

"Show me where it hurts."

Her hand reached behind her and her fingers tentatively traveled up the middle of her back. "Here. Is it bleeding?" she asked.

Through the thin material, silk if he had to

guess, there wasn't any blood seeping through. "No blood."

She exhaled. "Good. Bruising?"

Colby gingerly raised the fabric until he saw the lower outline of a purple bruise and then pulled the shirt back down. "Yes, you have a bruise."

"How big?" Regan asked.

Colby took a step back and held his breath in an attempt to get his heart to stop hammering against his ribs. "I don't know. It looks nasty, but not as bad as it could have been. The jacket saved you from a bigger injury."

Regan turned to face him. "You'd make a lousy doctor," she said, a frown on her face.

"And you'd make a lousy bounty hunter, so we're even."

"What makes you say that?"

"I don't know—hiding out at your own house with the goods you stole from the hospital, for one. For two, opening the door on the first knock."

Regan crossed her arms. "Point made."

Colby surveyed the scene around him. He didn't see anyone suspicious and he hadn't seen anyone following them. As soon as they'd fled on the bike, he was pretty sure he'd gained enough distance before their pursuers could even get in a vehicle to track them.

What was odd? No police seemed to be too interested in their presence. If local law enforcement had a BOLO, Colby and his bike would be easy to spot.

Were the police looking for them? And if not, why not? Why a military presence? Was it as Regan had said—Homeland Security? And if so, why was Nicholas Abrams, a man he'd served with as part of Delta Force, hunting Regan?

"Colby?" Her voice broke into his thoughts.

"Yes."

"Is your plan to stand out in the open in a parking lot all day? Because, if it is, I'm beginning to doubt your bounty hunter skills. Particularly with this bike out for all to see."

She was right. He was letting too many things distract him.

And the thing that was distracting him the most, he was tied to for the foreseeable future.

After parking the bike at the rear of the building, Colby pulled Regan's purse out of the saddlebag. They went inside and purchased a room with the cash she had. Once inside the less than ideal room that sported a queen-size bed and a pull-out couch, Colby used the room phone to call Dan to have him drop off a beat-up vehicle they often used for surveillance.

"I don't know if I like being your porter, but I'll like getting to take your baby for a ride today. Orange Crush—isn't that what you call it?" Dan asked.

"Just make sure you're not followed and bring me one of the bags I have locked in the safe."

"How serious is this, boss?"

Colby turned. Regan was still in the bathroom. "I don't know yet." He flipped on the television and scrolled through the channels. "Have you seen anything interesting on the news?"

"Such as?"

"A missing doctor? A missing virus?"

Dan exhaled sharply through the phone. "Do I need to be buying biohazard gear? Taping the window cracks with duct tape?"

"I don't think so. Not yet at least."

"You're never one to sugarcoat things. Once in a while—could you please try?"

"I'll see you soon. And I meant what I said. Make sure you're not followed—coming or going."

Regan stepped from the bathroom just as Colby discontinued the call. He kept the television on a local station to monitor anything breaking that could change their plans.

Regan sat on the edge of the bed while Colby took a seat on the threadbare couch. "What's the plan?" she asked.

"My associate is swapping our wheels for a

vehicle that won't draw nearly as much attention as the motorcycle. He's also bringing some cash and other necessary items for going off grid. Nontraceable phones and some other things."

Regan nodded, eyeing the cooler that sat on the cracked wood dresser. "As soon as we get that car, we need to go to my friend's lab and change out the vials. The samples need to stay frozen, but I think the dry ice packed in there should hold out until then."

"Right. And then to the drop-off point. I'd like to at least get a view of it before tomorrow night."

"Do you think...?" Her voice trailed off.

Colby knew what she wanted to ask. It didn't take any special knowledge to understand that the first person on her mind was her daughter. Even though Regan didn't discuss her at every moment, there was the impenetrable worried undertone in her gray-green eyes that spoke volumes. He'd carried that look himself during the years his wife had suffered through cancer treatment.

"I think Olivia is still alive," Colby said, hoping the determination in his voice would be enough to get her to believe. He needed her to have faith so she could do what needed to be done. If she gave up, Sam's life hung in the balance.

"How can you be sure?"

"Because they clearly want you alive, as well—which, to be honest, is what has me really worried."

She nodded without pressing him. Regan was a smart woman and even she could tell that if the bullet they'd fired had been a real one she could very well be dead.

That was when regular programming changed and the local television news anchor appeared on the screen. "Military personnel associated with the Department of Defense are looking for Regan and Olivia Lockhart—a local doctor and her eleven-year-old daughter. Dr. Lockhart's nanny, Polina Sokolov, has been found dead, presumably murdered." A photo of Regan and Olivia flashed on the screen, taken from the hospital's website from last year's Christmas party. "If you see either of these individuals, please contact local authorities immediately."

Regan covered her eyes and wept.

SIX

Regan sat in the beat-up car Colby had traded his motorcycle for and watched the road unfold in front of her. Colby drove, his hands firm and steady on the wheel, as she shook like a leaf next to him.

It was as if her life was now an overturned hourglass—each small piece of sand dripping down, taking minutes off not only her life but Olivia's, as well.

Polina was dead? Who were these people? Murdering someone went against one of her primary beliefs that she held most dear—that life was precious. To callously extinguish someone because they were in the way of a criminal goal was so foreign to her mind that it left her stomach a boiling mess of acrid liquid. If they could kill Polina so easily, what did that mean for Olivia?

Would any of them make it out alive?

"How much farther?" Colby asked.

Regan blinked and watched the green stakes

at the side of the road, waiting for the next mile marker. She gripped the cooler handle in her hands to ground her in the moment. She swallowed several times to try to clear the tightness from her throat without avail.

"I don't know. Maybe twenty minutes. I'm looking for the silo."

They'd been driving for a couple of hours. So far, they hadn't seen any law enforcement. One step Colby had taken was to dress Regan down in clothes from a local thrift store—trading her pressed business slacks and silk shirt for jeans and a black tank top covered by a plaid flannel shirt with darker hues of pink and purple. She'd pulled her auburn hair up into a ponytail and covered her head with a Denver Broncos baseball cap. A large pair of shades, and she hardly recognized herself in the mirror.

At least Colby hadn't been tied to Regan from what they could make out from the press coverage. Seemingly they weren't looking for him, which was good news for her.

They were driving east from Denver, leaving the mountains behind them for the agricultural fields of eastern Colorado.

"A silo?"

"Yes, a red one."

Brian Hollis, one of the researchers she used to work with, had gone into private business.

One of the perks had been building a lab for his special projects in rural Colorado. After they'd parted ways after a lab crisis, they had communicated little. He'd invited her once to his lab after the construction was complete, seemingly to want her opinion on its design, but then ended up hinting at the possibility of the two of them working together again. She hadn't encouraged him. Regan didn't necessarily want to know what he was now involved in. Brian, though good-natured, always had a secretive edge.

Minutes ticked by slowly. Regan scanned the horizon. A police car was approaching from the other direction.

Regan's heart seized. She felt light-headed. One thing she knew for sure, evading justice didn't soothe her temperament. Colby checked the speedometer. Even though he hadn't been speeding, it was everyone's instinct to check just to make sure they were not going over the limit.

He settled his hand on hers. "Deep breath. It's going to be fine. Just keep looking straight ahead."

Regan's heart galloped in her throat. The two cars passed. Colby's eyes drifted to the rearview mirror. "He's not braking. We're fine."

Regan exhaled and flexed her fingers to ease the muscle ache from gripping the cooler so tightly. She had to figure out some way to ease the stress or it was going to rip her apart. She needed her thoughts to be able to connect if she had any hope of getting Olivia back alive.

"I have to say, you make a really bad criminal."

"Isn't that a good thing?"

"Only if you want to be caught." He winked at her and opened his mouth to say something more when his eyes were pulled outside his window. "There." Colby pointed. "The red silo?"

Regan looked left. Yes, exactly as she remembered. "Turn here."

Colby turned off the highway and the car bumped along the road like a raft in white water.

"Another ten miles or so down this road," Regan said.

Colby nodded.

She'd give anything to be able to read his mind. What did he think of her? What did he think of this situation? He seemed all-in. He didn't talk much about Sam or if he was even worried about her. Just on task. His mind set. One goal at a time.

"Did you ever visit this Brian Hollis at this lab?" Colby asked.

"Years ago. Why?"

"Look." Colby pointed his finger, and Regan followed the line to a house that was charred, burned to the studs.

"No, it's not possible. Drive past the house. His lab was down the way—hidden in the trees."

They eased passed the blackened skeletal remains of the house, and Colby was able to fit the vehicle through a couple of stalwart pines to hide it at the back of the lab outbuilding. Colby parked the car and got out. Regan set the cooler at the base of passenger's foot well and got out of the car, as well. The air was still smoky—reminiscent of a neighborhood barbecue.

Colby took her hand and they walked to the building. It was still intact but sat as silent as death. How was it that the absence of human presence could be felt without definitive verification?

They stopped at the door. Colby tested the knob. It opened and they stepped through the door with small, stilted steps. Colby dropped Regan's hand, motioned her behind him and drew a small firearm.

No sound. The air was dry and stale, and it hurt to breathe. Each door they passed Colby opened and motioned for her to stay in the hall as he scouted the room.

Nothing. No person. The sound of a normally working lab was replaced with complete silence.

Colby opened the first set of clear glass doors to what appeared to be the main lab. At the second set, the lock on the wall had been destroyed and when Colby pushed through Regan didn't hear the whoosh that signified that air was being pulled into the lab—a negative pressure area. When working with pathogens, many lab spaces had special HEPA filters and vents that pulled air into the lab versus pushing it outside unfiltered, which would risk a pathogen infecting citizens in nearby communities. Regan shuddered. Hopefully she and Colby hadn't just inhaled something that could kill them.

Regan eased away from Colby and each flanked opposite sides of the room. Regan scanned the metal tables. Experiments suspended in progress. Open notebooks. The next set of worktables revealed an overturned chair, broken flasks and an unidentified yellow liquid that oozed over the floor. No discernible odor. Hopefully it was a benign spilled suspension liquid often used in medical experiments.

She leaned down for a closer look and that was when she saw the trail of blood. A hand settled on her shoulder and Regan cried out, nearly toppling forward into the red droplets and mysterious yellow fluid.

Colby gripped her shoulder and pulled her up. He stepped in front of her and they began to follow the crimson polka-dot trail.

Lord, please, don't let anyone be dead here. I

don't know what's happened, but please let everyone be okay. Let us find something to help Olivia.

The trail traveled outside the lab, down a hallway and eventually ended at a back door. Colby opened it and scanned the surrounding area. A set of tire tracks and spewed gravel littered the sidewalk. Colby closed and locked the door, grabbed the tail end of his shirt and polished the metal to erase his fingerprints.

"Better safe than sorry. Let's not make it easy for them to connect the two of us. My prints would be on file for my bounty hunter license."

"Smart."

"Let's go back into the lab and see if we can find something that will help us. I don't think it's a coincidence that your friend goes missing when we need somewhere to store a virus."

They entered the lab again. Regan headed to the corner of the room that housed four large freezers. The locks had been destroyed, as well. Her arms prickled. She opened the first one and pushed her hand into the vacant compartment, finding it warm with pooled water at the bottom.

The next two freezers were the same story. Empty and warm. Regan risked touching the pooled water. It was room temperature, but considering the water was still present and the house still smoldered, she reasoned whatever happened here had been in the last couple of days.

"Don't you think they would have been using them?" Colby asked. "Otherwise the doors would be open to keep them from rotting."

Regan nodded. She opened the fourth freezer. It, too, was no longer functioning. Inside were several vials and when she peered at the bottom there were some cracked and opened.

She slammed the door closed and shoved Colby away.

"What was it? What did you see?"

Regan covered her mouth and nose with the sleeve of her shirt until her lungs burned, and she inhaled deeply. Had she just killed them both by so recklessly exposing them to open vials of a substance she had no idea of what it could possibly contain? Everyone thought US labs operated at a certain safety level.

If only they knew.

Colby's skin crawled and he had an immediate desire to bathe himself in a tub of bleach. One of Regan's hands still gripped the freezer door—her knuckles as white as her face.

They stood there looking at one another. He exhaled slowly.

"What do we do?" Colby asked.

"If there was anything deadly in there that has an airborne transmission—it's probably too late for us."

Colby shoved his hands into his pockets. What he should have felt was anger. Dismay. What had he gotten himself into by agreeing to help this woman? Not every lost soul could be helped. Thoughts of Sam crept into his mind. If he didn't finish this he might as well dig her grave himself—so desperate was her fate without the cure Regan kept in that cooler.

Predominantly, Colby felt that Regan wasn't being on the level with him. The one man she wanted to secret away this virus to just to keep it safe was missing under mysterious circumstances. What did that mean? Was he a victim as much as Regan was?

Regan dropped her hand from the freezer's handle. "Let's look around some more. See if we can find any lab books that might shed light on what Brian and his staff were doing."

Colby followed her. Surrounding the central work area were some offices. Regan pointed him to one and she headed to the other.

"I don't think it's a good idea for me to go alone," Colby said.

"Why not? We can cover more ground if we split up."

What she said was true, but if he were honest with himself, he'd have to confess he was having doubts about the veracity of Regan's story. He couldn't wash away the thought that something, clearly, more nefarious was going on. People didn't torch houses unless they were trying to make a point.

"It's just that I don't really know what you're looking for."

"Lab notebooks—usually they're composition notebooks. The same kind kids buy for school." She stared at him and then motioned him to follow her into the first office.

The drawers had already been rifled through. No notebooks. Regan began to go through the papers strewed across the floor.

"Those don't look like notebooks."

She looked up at him. "They're receipts."

"And that helps us how?"

Regan ignored him as she gathered up and then leafed through the papers. She pulled one out, dropped the rest, and stood. "Did you know you can buy viruses?"

Colby swallowed heavily. "Like what kind?"

"Any kind, if you know the right people."

"Deadly viruses?"

"Of course. Ebola. HIV. Marburg."

"And that's legal?"

"All depends on what your purpose is. The US military needs these lethal viruses to do research on how to develop countermeasures like vaccines."

"Or build weapons."

Regan shook her head. "Manufacturing bioweapons is against the law."

"Sure," Colby said.

"It is."

"People do things regardless of whether or not it's against the law. Why do you think I have a job?"

She turned and sidled up to him. Her bare forearm touched his and a soothing comfort spread through him. "They were buying wild polio virus."

"For what?"

"I don't know, but as long as you're vaccinated, there's probably nothing here that will sicken us. It gives me an idea. We can take some of the intact vials from the freezer and switch them for the ones I took from the hospital. There's probably some dry ice around here so we can replenish what's in the cooler. We just need to take the vials from the hospital and hide them somewhere where they'll stay frozen. Somewhere safe to protect the cure."

"Like where?"

"Somewhere these criminals won't think to look."

Colby rubbed his face with his hand. Where could that be? "Any ideas?"

"I was thinking of some friends I have at other hospitals but they're also competitors. I don't know if I would trust them to keep their hands off what's in the case."

"Does it have to be a fancy freezer?"

She shook her head. "Standard."

Who could Colby trust that would never be tied to him? His former mother-in-law? They had a good relationship.

"How do you know Brian?"

Regan's eyes widened. "What?"

Something smart almost slipped off his tongue. She'd heard him for sure. Why the delay tactic? "How do you know this guy?"

"We used to work together. I was head of a private lab once."

"Why did you leave?"

"I was being recruited by several hospitals who were offering me very lucrative contracts. I was a single mom."

"More money than the private sector? I find that hard to believe."

Regan slumped into an office chair. "There was an accident while I was there. Several people died."

Colby's throat tightened. He leaned against the wall to hide the fact her statement made him weak in the knees. "How?"

"It was never really determined."

"But I'm sure you have some theories on the matter," Colby challenged.

"I really can only speculate. Let's see if we can find anything else in the other offices."

Shut down. Clearly she didn't want to continue discussing it. Colby, however, couldn't let it go. What if what had happened in that lab had every bearing on what was happening to them now?

The last two offices didn't hold any information—at least none that Regan seemed to be interested in.

Regan, much more confidently this time, opened the freezer that held the mysterious vials, scanned the labels on the tubes and grabbed half a dozen. They found a waist high freezer with dry ice, put some in a bag, and walked back to the car.

"How long ago was this?" Colby asked.

"What?"

"This accident at your lab?"

"Over ten years ago."

"What did the investigation find?"

Regan reached the car and pulled the door open but stared at him over the top of the beat-up hood. "Why are you so determined to talk about this? It was a very painful time for me. What's in the past should be left there. I'm not asking you to go back and dig up everything you'd like to keep buried."

She ducked down and got into the car. He climbed in, as well.

"You don't think it might be relevant to what's going on right now? Especially since someone you worked with is also missing? His house has been burned down. The two of you being targeted makes me look at how the two of you were tied together, and it was working at that lab."

"Three lab workers died. Their respiratory systems seized up."

"What?"

"Something caused instant muscular paralysis. If your diaphragm doesn't move—then you basically suffocate to death."

"And the cause?"

"It could have been that the polio virus became aerosolized somehow, but that was never proved. Polio can transmit via the air, but those workers had been vaccinated, so even they shouldn't have suffered any ill effects from the virus leaking out. A mutated, highly virulent form of polio must have infected them."

"Is that what you think?"

"I don't know… I honestly don't know."

Was she telling him the truth? She opened the cooler and stuck the vials and ice inside. "What's next?" she asked, her tone ending any interrogation on his part.

"First, we hide the cure and then go to the park and have a look around before the exchange tomorrow night."

SEVEN

It had been years since Colby had seen his mother-in-law, Denise. Her surprise at his unexpected arrival didn't hinder her warm reception of both him and Regan.

"Colby, I'm so surprised to see you here."

Regan walked in behind him but as soon as she shook Denise's hand there was clear recognition on her face.

"You're the doctor they're looking for. They think that you murdered someone."

"Let's talk." Colby quickly ushered Denise into her living room. Though he didn't suspect anyone was following them, he parted the curtain and peered out the front of the house just to be sure.

Empty.

"Colby, what's going on? I don't hear from you for years and then you show up at my door with a wanted woman."

Perhaps Colby had misread the quality of their

relationship. Now, he wondered about how wise his choice had been. Too late now.

"I'm sorry. I know I should have been better about keeping in touch."

"Yes, you should have." Pain etched her voice.

Colby's heart fell like a rock. His eyes captured Regan's, and she turned away from him and began scanning the photographs Denise had on the mantel above her fireplace.

Tears welled in Denise's eyes and she quickly wiped at them—her movements brisk. "You're the only connection I have left to my daughter."

"She's beautiful," Regan said.

Colby felt relief wash over him. Regan would be better at this type of conversation. She was a doctor, after all—she was practiced at managing uncomfortable situations.

"Tell me about her," Regan said.

"Brook was one of the most fascinating people you'd ever meet. She was very calm and peaceful. Yoga instructor. Massage therapist. She always wanted to make people feel better. I never thought Colby was a great fit for her, but he slowly changed my mind. He was so protective."

Did grief ever fully go away? Just hearing Denise speak about Brook brought back a wave of emotion. Things he'd stuffed down for years. Thought he'd dealt with. Healed from.

Should he still feel this way?

"I'm sorry that she died so young," Regan said. "Cancer—such an awful disease."

Regan's eyebrows shot up.

He read her mind in that instant and knew she likely felt betrayed that he hadn't shared that piece of information with her.

"How is Sam?" Denise directed the question at Colby.

"Sam is partly why we're here," Colby said. "Dr. Lockhart developed a cure for Sam's type of brain cancer, but some bad people are after her. What you see in the news is a lie. She's not responsible for her nanny's death. Her daughter is being held for ransom for what's inside this cooler. We'd like to leave it here…to protect it."

Denise settled herself on the couch. Heaviness settled throughout Colby's body. He hadn't been fair to Denise and now his absence from her life could cost him the help he needed.

Regan cleared her throat. "I know this is asking a lot. More than anyone should ever ask of a stranger…at least to me, but above all I want to protect this cure for other patients. If you don't hear from us in seven days, I want you to stick the vials in a cooler like this one with some dry ice and take it back to Strang Memorial. They'll know what to do with it."

"Even without you?" The words slipped from Colby's mouth before his mind had formed the thought. Why did he challenge her? Or was it even a challenge at all?

"They'll find a way." Regan turned back to Denise. "Will you help us? I know that I don't have anyone else to turn to, and Colby thinks you're our best hope."

"What happens when the police figure out that Colby is helping you?" Denise asked. "Won't they come here? Checking family first?"

In truth, he hadn't teased out all the potential possibilities. The scenario playing out in front of him was odd in the least and not having experience in hiding a wanted woman made it less possible to rely on his experience. He had to undo his training and think opposite of how he normally thought.

It wasn't a comfortable space to be in.

Denise was at risk. If they tied Colby to Regan, then of course they would look into all of his known associates. Dead wife or not, they'd talk to Denise at some point.

"You need to give the cooler to someone else. Someone you trust but that I've never met," Colby said.

Regan shook her head. "No, I'm not willing to take that chance." Regan turned to Denise. "Listen, you are putting yourself in danger. I'm worried that the more people are involved, the more at risk their lives will be and the higher the chance the cure could be lost."

Colby folded his hands together and leaned forward. "Perhaps we're putting too much emphasis on the importance of these vials. The cure can be made again."

"Of course it can, but not manufactured in enough time to save Sam. And if something happens to me, it could delay this treatment for years to come. I have notes, but to protect this intellectual property I've left gaps in those documents to prevent a competitor from stealing it."

Colby inhaled, and tension caused his neck to ache. Did the criminals intend to put them between a rock and a hard place?

Of course, that was the goal of every criminal.

"I'll do it," Denise said.

Both Colby and Regan zeroed in on Denise.

"If ultimately whatever is in this cooler will help people suffering from cancer, then I want to help. No parent should have to go through what I've gone through—burying a child." She turned to Colby, a measure of resolve in her eyes. "A young marriage shouldn't end in the manner yours did. So much was taken away when Brook died. I'll do what I can to give back—even if it could mean trouble for me."

* * *

After their long day yesterday, Regan and Colby had crashed at the hotel and decided scoping out the park would be better in the morning after they were rested and well fed.

Regan surrendered to the pull of Colby's hand and nestled her prone body next to him in the dirt. He pulled out a set of binoculars and scanned the area. The day was bright—a morning where parents could expect to play with their children in a park uninterrupted by criminal happenings. And here it would come to pass in a few short hours that she would trade her daughter for an active polio virus. At least, she assumed that was what was now present in those vials.

Regan's stomach was in knots. Having this virus was risky. It put the community at risk if it didn't stay frozen in that cooler. Everything about this play area reminded her of what she'd missed with Olivia. She hadn't been the type of mother to take Olivia to the park—to watch her gallivant around and try the monkey bars and jungle gyms under her watchful eye. It was hard not to feel guilty for those lost times, but she didn't think she had wasted her time. Life was a balance and as much as she yearned to change her approach with Olivia, would anyone else have come up with the cure she had?

The teeter-totter swayed in the wind as if two

invisible children played. That tilting of one end up and down was so much like life. A decision always had consequences. Even good decisions could have bad outcomes.

If she got Olivia back, there had to be a way to change her trajectory with her daughter. The look in Denise's eyes at remembering all those lost moments with her daughter had been a knife of conviction straight into Regan's gut.

Lord, I know I probably haven't been all that Olivia has needed, but You gifted her to me for a reason. Please, help Colby and me get her back safely. Above all, keep her safe until I can figure out a way to get her back.

Colby took her hand and squeezed it. "You okay?" he asked, his voice a shade under his normal tone.

"Could be better," Regan confessed.

"We'll get her back."

"Promise?"

"Promise."

His words sounded even and sure, though her body still trembled despite the warm day. Her training taught her to always consider the worst-case scenario first but going down that path in her mind when it involved Olivia's life was something she couldn't do. It was time to just work the problem one step at a time.

"Do you see anything?" Regan asked.

"Swings. A teeter-totter." He smiled at her—a clear attempt at humor to lighten her spirits.

"I mean—"

"I know." He hunkered down and scanned the area again. "Nothing out of place. Maybe you should take a look."

Regan took the binoculars from him. She, too, didn't see anything out of the ordinary.

"What's your plan?" Regan asked.

"I think we'll approach the park down that road." Colby pointed, and Regan looked that way through the magnifiers. "There're a couple of different dirt roads that jut off from the main one. More possibilities for escape."

Regan handed the binoculars back. "Do you think they'll just give Olivia back?"

Colby shrugged. "I don't know. I'm worried. If Polina were just missing or found alive somewhere, I'd feel a lot better about this whole deal. Keeping the real cure from them might actually help us. I don't see them harming anyone until they know for sure that they have what they want."

"They'll test it to be sure."

"That will take a little time, right? Which gives us exactly what we need. More time to work the problem. Keeping Olivia alive keeps you working for them. If they harm her, then there's no reason for you to cooperate."

"You make it sound like they're going to take me. That this is just a ruse to flush me out with the virus."

"It's true. I have my doubts as to whether or not they'll let us go with Olivia."

"What do you think will happen?"

"I wish I could predict. If they take you, I'll follow. I think we need to set our minds on the fact that today isn't going to be the end. Too much is still in play. They'll have to verify you held up your end of the bargain."

"If you could guess…what would your best guess be?"

"I think they'll try and take you…and I don't think you should put up much of a fight."

EIGHT

Regan's heart thudded wildly at the base of her throat as Colby parked the car a few blocks away from the park. They'd grabbed a quick bite of fast food, which sat clumped in Regan's gut. The sun was just beginning to hide behind the distant Rocky Mountains, its light casting differentiating shadows among the peaks, giving them the illusion of being one-dimensional paper cutouts of varying shades of blue.

Normally, viewing the sunset was a welcome respite for Regan. It meant the day was done, and she regularly watched the beautiful moment to help put perspective into her day—often from one of the upper floors of the hospital if she hadn't made it home yet. Dealing with people who were in the throes of a medical crisis definitely took a toll that was rarely spoken of. The emotional currency spent on helping patients sometimes left little for other family relationships. Every bit of her reserve was given to Olivia.

Had they hurt her daughter? Would Olivia be the same as she was before?

Would any of them be the same?

"You okay?" Colby asked.

His voice pulled Regan's gaze from the window, and she studied the calm demeanor of his face. His blue eyes were soft, questioning. His brown hair tousled but seemingly every strand in its proper place.

Smiling faintly, he reached for her hand, which held thc cooler in her lap. Her skin tingled under his touch and, for a moment, she couldn't resist staying locked in his gaze. The comfort there was something she found in few other people. The message without words seemed to be "all will be well."

"I know it's a weird question considering the circumstances we find ourselves in, but I need your head in the game."

She looked back out the window. "I'm okay, considering."

He dropped his hand, and she wished that he hadn't, but taking his hand back seemed too forward and inappropriate considering the circumstances.

Circumstances and games. Is that what life boiled down to? What different choices could she have made to prevent her from experiencing this right now? If she'd chosen differently, would someone else have come up with a cure for glioblastoma? Would she and Olivia have a closer, deeper relationship?

Would she have met Colby?

Her faith taught her that nothing was a coincidence. That God was the energy behind everything. Each sunrise and sunset. Each breath. Each heartbeat.

If that were true, then in some measure all these things were supposed to happen for some reason. Or there was the other tenet. God uses all things for good.

But how could that be possible in this situation?

What she didn't want to confess was how much she was beginning to rely on Colby. How she didn't want to take a step forward without his guidance. She trusted him to get her through this even if his motive was only to save Sam.

Whatever happened in the end with Colby, as long as Olivia was alive and physically unharmed, Regan could take as long as all they both needed were to pick up the mental pieces.

Colby tapped his watch—his fingernail against the glass like someone sliding the tip of a cool knife up her spine. "It's time. You should get into position."

Regan placed her right hand on the door, looking back at him. "Where will you be?"

"Close. I don't want to tell you because I don't want you to accidentally give my position away. Just do as I instructed. Give them the cooler and get your hands on Olivia. Don't let her go. Hopefully, they'll just drive away and then we'll go straight to the police and report what happened."

"And if that doesn't happen?"

"I'll help any way I can. The situation will be fluid, as they say, but I'm not going to abandon you. The goal for tonight, for right now, is just to get Olivia back unharmed. We'll deal with the rest after that happens."

Not you but we.

That statement of camaraderie strengthened Regan's resolve, and she opened the door and stepped out.

Colby grabbed her wrist and locked her eyes with his. "Just...stay safe. Okay?"

She nodded and eased the door closed. Turning, she began to walk toward the park like a soldier on a mission. Her stomach felt like a block of ice. Her head buzzed, trying to plan contingencies for all the possibilities that could happen.

Is this some of what Colby felt when he'd headed into battle?

Nighttime at the park was flat-out creepy. The playground equipment resembled tortured, twisted metal. The cool wind bit at Regan's skin and she pulled the flannel shirt tight around her frame. She stood alone, the cooler gripped between two hands, in the middle of the park. Time flowed as slowly as cold honey. Regan both wished for and yet resisted the movement of time. While they had been waiting, Olivia was alive.

At least, Regan hoped beyond hope that she was.

Lord, please bring my daughter back to me in one piece. Don't let them have harmed her in any way. Bring us out of this alive.

The sound of tires traversing gravel made every muscle in Regan's body tense. Her body was priming her emergency response system. Run. Fight. Freeze.

Which one would it ultimately be?

The car came into view, and Regan inhaled deeply to try to stem the rapid galloping of her heartbeat. Her ears tingled at every sound and her mind tried to split those sounds to see if any were evidence of Colby drawing closer.

The car was now in full view. The windows were tinted darker than legally allowed. A four-door sedan.

Regan widened her stance to keep from toppling over and clutched the cooler to her abdomen to prevent her ill-advised dinner from traveling up and out.

The car stopped and killed its engine.

And then…just sat there.

Nothing moved. The night was as silent as the hospital morgue at midnight.

Regan bit into her lip. What was she supposed to do, exactly? Approach the car? Wait?

She squared her shoulders and dropped the cooler to the ground. If they wanted it, they'd have to come get it.

The door opened, its hinges creaking like every storybook haunted house before the maniacal serial killer came out wielding a bloody knife.

Regan folded her hands together to steady their shaking.

A man stood. Even with her eyes adjusted to the darkness, it was hard for Regan to make out his features. He wore sunglasses and had a ball cap pulled low.

"Dr. Lockhart, good of you to join us this evening."

"Where is my daughter? Where is Olivia?"

"First, I need you to walk the cooler over here."

Colby's presumption came to the forefront of her mind—that what these men really wanted was her, as well. She couldn't let that happen. Regan picked up the cooler and began to walk backward, away from the car. It wasn't what Colby had advised, but felt right to her in the moment.

"I'm not going anywhere with this cooler until

I see that my daughter is alive. If I were you, I'd pull her out of that car right now."

Regan stopped and clenched her fists. Her voice stronger than she felt—a steely edge to it she'd never heard before. Pure anger and fear fueled by a seemingly open-ended stream of stress hormones.

The back door of the car opened and another man got out, leaned down and pulled a figure from the back of the car.

Regan's knees almost buckled. Though she couldn't see clearly, everything about the child's silhouette and demeanor cried to every cell in her mother's body that Olivia was alive.

At least for the moment.

Regan pressed her lips together. She picked the cooler up and walked farther back. Her goal was to get enough distance between them for her and Olivia to run once Regan had a hold of her—the cooler far enough away that they'd be more concerned with grabbing it and its contents to hopefully give Regan enough time to scurry away with her daughter.

"Dr. Lockhart, that's not wise," the man called to her.

She stopped. The end of the road evidently.

"This stays back here. Olivia and I will meet in the middle. Once I have her then you can do whatever you want with the cooler."

The man turned away from her and conversed with the other figure that had emerged from the back of the vehicle.

They muscled Olivia to walk toward Regan.

The distance between them seemed impossibly far apart. Regan left the cooler and walked to her daughter, watching every nuance of her steps to discern if she was okay. Olivia's hair was tangled, frizzy. Her shoulders shuddered from crying.

Colby's instructions swarmed through Regan's mind. *Walk slowly. Keep your wits about you. Look for anything that seems off...seems dangerous.*

Regan's love for Olivia dispelled any measure of safety and Regan broke into a run toward her daughter, her arms outstretched, her feet pummeling the dirt path.

A few steps away from Olivia, a sharp crack broke the still night. A sharp pain in Regan's neck stopped her cold. She reached up and felt not blood, but something cold and metallic sticking out from her flesh.

She yanked it. Her vision blurred and she fell to her knees.

Olivia, sweet Olivia, closed the distance and wrapped her arms around her mother, weeping, unable to speak words except, "I'm sorry."

Regan wanted to wrap her arms around her

daughter. To comfort her. To speak words that would reassure her that everything was going to be okay. But her arms didn't respond to the urgent impulses from her brain and her words came out like jumbled alphabet soup.

Regan slumped to the ground.

"Mom. Mom!" Olivia's eyes were wild with fear as her head hovered above her.

Run. Run! The words a moan from her lips. Her vision spun wildly and she clenched her eyes to avoid the sensation of falling over a cliff.

"Olivia! Run!"

Not her voice.

Colby's.

Colby watched, his face hot, as Regan did everything he'd instructed her not to do. Taunting criminals at a ransom drop-off had to be the first thing listed on what not to do when dealing with the underbelly of society.

He'd positioned himself approximately four hundred yards away under the small shield of three pine trees. Not great cover but enough for the little light that remained. He'd seen the car drive in off the main road.

Even from that distance, every mannerism of Regan's body beaconed fear. Her rigid, shaky stance. Her straightforward stare. Her head barely moving side to side to see if any other threat was present.

Which was why when she ran straight toward Olivia, she didn't see one of the two men raise his weapon at her, the shot off before Colby could even blink.

He broke from the trees as Regan reached for her neck and fell to her knees.

"Olivia! Run!"

Regan's daughter looked but didn't respond to his command. Colby raised his weapon and fired three successive shots over the heads of the kidnappers. Instead of turning tail and fleeing, they hunkered down behind their open car doors.

Colby was in open field with no cover to duck behind. He was ten steps away from Regan when the first projectile whistled past his ear.

He dove into the ground, sliding right next to Regan. Olivia was shaking her mom, attempting to wake her up. Colby fired three more shots in the direction of the car, mostly to keep them pinned until a plan came to fruition in his mind.

Olivia backed away from him. Could he blame her? She didn't know if he was good or bad. For all she knew, he was simply some deranged man screaming her name from the copse of a few trees. After all, she'd already been kidnapped. Had she also witnessed what happened to

Polina? Colby reached forward and pulled Olivia to the ground.

"Stay down. I'm a friend of your mom's."

"Is she dead?" Her voice was more whimper than question.

Colby shook his head—more as a wish than a statement of fact. He didn't know. Didn't want it to be true. Not only for Olivia's sake.

But his own.

He placed his hand on Regan's chest and felt a faint rise confirm her breathing. The distance between them and the car was perhaps a mere two hundred feet, but how did he get Regan, currently incapacitated, likely drugged, and her daughter to safety? He glanced back to the white-and-red cooler that was equally as far away.

He fired a round at the cooler. A glancing blow but it knocked it over.

"Whoever you are—that's not a wise decision."

"If you want the cooler, the three of us get to go."

"Then start walking."

"Let me see you!" Colby yelled. "Walk away from the car—hands up."

A faint shock rolled through Colby's body when they complied.

Something's not right here. That was too fast. Too easy.

Against his better judgment, Colby holstered his weapon. He scooped up Regan and settled her over his shoulder.

They want to take her, which is why they drugged her. They're not letting us out of here. I'm missing something.

Holding Regan's body with one arm, he held his other hand out for Olivia. "Please, take my hand."

She was shaking, crying. How could he build trust with this young girl under these circumstances?

"Olivia, take my hand right now. I won't hurt you. I'm trying to help."

She reached her hand out with tentative fingers and he clutched it quickly, before she could change her mind, and began to walk backward, slowly. Olivia's steps faltered beside his, a physical expression of the uncertainty in her mind.

The two men stayed where they were with their hands raised. Colby picked up his pace.

He felt the sting to his arm before he heard the sound. The two men never moved. Someone else. Someone else had been waiting. Watching.

"Looks like we beat you here!" one of the two men yelled.

Whatever the drug was, it didn't take long to course through his system and affect his muscles.

He staggered and, before he dropped Regan entirely, fell to his knees and laid her on the ground.

Olivia screamed as he fell. With sloppy, uncontrolled movements, he reached up and felt the dart but didn't have the strength to remove it.

Too late anyway.

His hand flopped across his body for his weapon. The motion drained every last vestige of energy, his head swimming violently, so much worse than when Regan had tased him.

Just before he lost consciousness, he heard gravel crunching beneath footsteps as the two men from the car approached.

"The early bird gets the worm as they say. Guess you weren't early enough."

NINE

The first sensation that registered in Regan's mind was a bone-chilling coldness like she was lying on a slab of ice. Her eyes were heavy, unable to open despite her attempts. She tried to lift her cheek away from the cold, and it immediately fell back onto an unforgiving, hard surface.

Time was fuzzy. If she had to guess—she'd say it was the next morning. Day three of her life upending itself.

She pressed her hands down and attempted a feeble push-up. The strength required, she didn't possess. Her world swam violently as if she was being held captive in a dinghy as it was violently being tossed in hurricane-fueled waves. She swallowed what little moisture she held in her mouth over a tongue that felt two times larger than normal. Her lips were dry and cracked.

Forcing her eyes open didn't improve her situation. The room was dark. Was it night? Was it the same night? She smoothed her hand over the cement, away from her, until it bumped against something warm and squishy.

Blood?

She blinked her eyes several times and soon she was able to discern the shape of a head in the darkness within arm's reach. She walked her hand out farther, touching skin that felt like coarse sandpaper. She walked her fingers up slowly—more tacky fluid.

Colby. A cut to his forehead.

She pushed up onto her elbows and shimmied next to him, the small movement sapping her strength. Her last memory came to the forefront of her mind and she reached with tentative fingers and brushed them along the side of her neck. The projectile was missing. In its place, a small crusted hill of dried blood.

She reached out for his shoulder and shook it—more than a gentle nudging. "Colby," she whispered. She army-crawled closer and laid her head on his chest. His breathing was slow, rhythmic. Likely enough to keep his oxygen levels up. Regan pulled his arm across her body and nestled her fingers in the groove of his wrist to feel for a pulse.

It was strong and steady under her touch.

Just like he was.

Likc no other man she'd ever known.

Drugs were funny things. Each person had

some degree of variance as to how they would react. If Regan fashioned a guess as to what the kidnappers' drug of choice had been, she'd put forth ketamine as the answer. However, ketamine was relatively short-acting. Depending on the dose, it might incapacitate a person for thirty to forty-five minutes. Too short to pick the two of them up, grab Olivia, and bring them to this place unless it was close to the location of the park. What other medication had they used to prolong their downtime?

Trouble was, this place felt empty and hollow. Like they'd been dropped into the bottom of an abandoned well, though from what she could see it looked like a large cage—dark, black lines jutted from the floor to the ceiling. The faint smell of rusty metal hung in her nose.

Where was Olivia? Was she here in this place? Was she safe? Still alive?

A lump formed at the base of Regan's throat. She bit her lip to prevent the tears from flowing. Had this been the right way to handle the situation? Or had she made every wrong choice along the way, putting Olivia's life at risk, as well as Colby's and all of her patients'? Should she have gone to the police right away?

Lord, I don't know the answer to all of these questions. I'm scared. Please, keep Olivia safe. Wake Colby up. Show us a way out of this prison.

She sniffed back tears, and Colby's body stirred next to hers. She turned onto her side and snuggled closer to him, holding his arm around her body, keeping her fingers pressed gently against his pulse as some sort of measure on his physical condition.

It wouldn't surprise her if these criminals had used an additional drug dose on Colby once he was down. He was bigger—stronger. They wouldn't have difficulty subduing Regan, even in the absence of the drug, but Colby would have been a different story.

Closing her eyes, she tried to focus on what she remembered. She'd seen Olivia—alive. They'd kept her safe. But taking Regan alive meant they wanted her for something and this event that had upended her life was far from over.

A snort—snoring? But Colby's body was still under her head. Nothing but the quiet rise and fall of his chest.

Another sound. Like someone clearing mucus from their throat. Regan lifted her head and narrowed her eyes against the darkness. The black lines were interrupted. She widened her eyelids, drinking in every molecule of light to discern the shape in the distance.

A man sitting in the corner—propped up? Seemingly drugged like she and Colby had been. She gripped Colby's hand tighter, almost willing the pressure to pull him out of his slumber. When that didn't work, she elbowed him against the ribs.

He moaned and turned on his side.

The man on the other side of the cage reached up and scratched his nose.

That made her think of the side effects of opiate narcotics like fentanyl, which could make people's noses itch. When an opiate was combined with ketamine it prolonged the sedative effects. Had that been the other drug they'd use to keep them down?

That was unknown, but what was known was that Regan and Colby were not alone in their cell.

A spark of pain along Colby's right ribs forced his eyes open. The world felt heavy. There was something pressing against his chest, making it hard for him to breathe. He knocked his head backward to force his senses to move more rapidly toward wakefulness and was met not with the soft surface of a pillow but cement. He reached his hand up and palpated the weight on his chest, first touching hair, then skin, then something cold and wet.

A hand gripped his tightly. "Colby, you're poking my eye."

Regan's voice. Merely a whisper. She lifted up her head. He blinked again, confirming his eyes were open. The darkness was deep. Where were they? He could make out steel bars, cold cement and little else.

A cell? A prison?

Whatever they'd hit him with felt like something he'd never experienced—even during some misguided days in his young adult life where alcohol seemed fun until the next morning. Only one or two episodes of that had taught him that was no way to feel. He hated that feeling.

Now it was a hundred times worse.

"Colby? Can you hear me?" Regan asked.

He could, but her whispers were drowned out by the jackhammer working on his brain. His forehead felt like it could explode off his body at any moment. He reached up and felt dried blood. Had they hit him with something to keep him unconscious longer? Hopefully, he'd put up a fight trying to save Regan and Olivia, and that was the cause of his injury.

"Colby!"

He winced, her words like daggers in his ears. The pain, the most intense he'd ever experienced. Even the migraines he'd suffered in the desert from dehydration and battle stress didn't compare to this.

He better answer her before she took drastic action. "I'm here." He groped for his watch. The kidnappers had taken it.

"Your head. I think it's cut open. There's a lot of blood."

That explained partly why he felt like he'd been on the losing end of a fight. He shifted to his side but had to lay his head down for the vertigo to subside. Never in such a short time had he been injured so much. First tased. Now drugged. Perhaps pistol-whipped to the head to keep him down longer.

What he could never say was that life with Regan was boring.

"Where are we?" he asked.

"Keep your voice down. There's someone else here."

He pushed up onto his elbow. "Where?"

"In the cell with us."

Another prisoner? "Who?"

"I don't know. It's too dark. I can't make his face out."

Colby sat up and crossed his legs to give himself a steady base. His body cried for sleep—real sleep. Not this concussion, drug-induced haze he was battling through. Colby squinted and could make out the shape in the distance. "Hey!"

Regan put her hand over his mouth like he was a wayward child. "What are you doing?"

Colby pulled her hand down. "Trying to find out if he's alive."

There was no movement from the man.

"He's probably been drugged like we were."

Colby shrugged. Did he want to go over there and check? What could he do at the moment? Honestly, he didn't feel well. From what he could tell, there didn't appear to be anything to sleep on.

"Let's just rest. He's obviously not a threat at the moment. He's a prisoner like us. We can't do anything right now until there's light, or people or something. But what we can do is rest."

Colby scooted back against a wall, and she sat next to him. He inched her forward, putting his arm around her shoulders and pulling her closer. For warmth? He wasn't sure in the moment, but she willingly allowed the closeness and nestled herself against his chest.

It had been a long time since he'd had a woman so close to him. After his wife and unborn baby had died, he'd dated a few other women, but hadn't found any emotional connection. Regan was different in ways he found hard to express with words. Maybe it was the push-away-no-please-help-me quality that complicated so many relationships between men and women.

Right now with Regan next to him, even considering their current predicament, a lot felt right with the world. If God destined certain events to happen, then there was reason and purpose behind their meeting. With Colby's skill set, he was the perfect person to get involved in a situation such as Regan's. He lived close to the edge of the law but never over it. Regan pushed the boundaries of her field enough to come up with a solution to one of the most devastating cancers that afflicted the human race. Two personality peas from the same pod.

A small shudder raced through Regan's body, and Colby cupped her head with his hand, brushing his fingers over her hair. Colby suspected she'd drifted off to sleep. He'd often wondered how people in these situations could sleep, but his body begged for it.

How was Sam? Was she okay? Was she still alive? His mother was probably rife with worry. Had the police paired him and Regan together? What did the public think about Regan right now? That she'd murdered her nanny? And if they believed that, would the medical board ever let Regan practice medicine again?

At first, the solution to Regan's problem seemed simple. Get Olivia back. Deliver a placebo that could hopefully pass well enough for the real thing—at least long enough for them to escape. Get Regan back to the hospital with the real deal—the true cure. Save Sam.

But now, the layers of this crisis were beyond anything Colby could have imagined. What was his old military friend turned nemesis doing at

Regan's house? Who was this other man drugged in their cage? Seemingly not a cell, as it had nothing to sleep on and smelled faintly of musty, wet canine.

Colby leaned his head against the concrete and just as he closed his eyes…

Someone turned on the lights.

TEN

Colby's body jerked, and Regan's eyes flew open as their world whitewashed. She covered her eyes with her hands and felt Colby stand next to her. Slowly, she inched her hands away, allowing varying degrees of light in until her pupils constricted from the dark world they'd opened themselves up to.

It was as if she and Colby had landed in a foreign country. Realistically they could be in a foreign country. At least she didn't think so. Regan struggled to her feet, brushing the dirt and leaves from her pants, eventually giving up when she realized what a futile gesture it was in her current state.

Colby took her hand gently in his and took a step forward in a protective stance.

A man stood in front of them dressed in black cargo pants and a black T-shirt. His face was uncovered and a look of displeasure creased his features, some sort of automatic weapon strapped crosswise against his body. He was bald, clean-shaved, with mean almost-black eyes. There was a black cobra tattooed onto the back of his right hand.

"About time you woke up. Well, at least two of you."

For the first time, Regan got a clear look at the other man in the cage. It was Brian Hollis. Had they burned down his house as a threat and then taken him? Where was the rest of his staff? Why was he there? What did they want them to do?

Regan turned back to the hostage-taker. "Where's my daughter?"

Baldy raised a finger and wiggled it back and forth like he was warning a wayward child. "You, Dr. Lockhart, haven't been following directions very well. What I can tell you is Olivia is safe for the time being, but if you don't start doing as you're asked, then all that will change."

"I want to see her," Regan demanded.

"Give us something we want and we'll return the favor. So far, you've made this whole process very difficult."

Another man approached, holding a cardboard box. Same stocky build but with black hair and vibrant green eyes. Baldy took his weapon and aimed it their way. Colby moved Regan behind him. Would he really take a bullet for her?

"Step to the back of the cell," Baldy ordered.

They complied and he let the weapon drop so he could unlock the door. Then Green Eyes slid the box across the concrete, and the door was quickly closed and locked.

"When everyone's awake, we'll talk. The sooner you can make that happen, Dr. Lockhart, perhaps we'll let you see your daughter. Just know—there are no guarantees," Baldy said, offering a snarl to add credence to his threat. Then they both walked away.

Colby dropped her hand and neared the box. At this juncture Regan doubted there was anything dangerous in it. Why kill them now when they seemed intent on keeping them alive for some purpose? He lifted the flaps and motioned her over.

It was filled with medical supplies and some food.

"First, we need to check Brian."

Colby raised an eyebrow. "You know him?"

Regan walked to Brian and kneeled next to him. "This is the man who owns the lab we went to." She settled her hand on his shoulder and shook him gently. "Brian. It's Regan Lockhart. Can you hear me?"

"You want this?" Colby asked, holding up a stethoscope. Interesting addition to the box. Any medical provider worth their salt should be able to tell if a patient was breathing and had a heartbeat without one.

She held her hand up and Colby walked over. "Looks like they worked him over pretty good."

Regan put the eartips in her ears and applied the bell to Brian's chest. Heartbeat steady. Breathing even but shallow. She looped the stethoscope around her neck and gently pulled his eyelids open. The pupils constricted normally.

With light fingers, she palpated his face to see if any of the bones appeared broken around the bruising. Without an X-ray she couldn't be sure, but the bones were in a normal position and didn't shift under her touch. She examined the skin around his neck and couldn't discern an injection site. Nothing on his arms until she examined the skin at the bend of Brian's right elbow and saw what she presumed was a needle mark. No bruising at the site.

Interesting.

"What's wrong?" Colby asked.

"With him? Concussion probably. There's a lot of bruising to his face. Could be partly why he's not woken up yet."

"No, I meant why do you have that look on your face?"

"What look?"

"Like you're bothered by something you

found. Doctors always have that look when they're thinking something but they don't necessarily want to share it."

Could Colby discern her looks so easily or did this come from the time he'd been forced to spend with doctors during his wife's and sister's illnesses?

"The injection mark here…" Regan tapped Brian's skin. "It seems like an odd place for someone unwilling to be drugged."

"What do you mean?"

Regan stood. "Think about where we were hit. My neck. Your arm. With a dart. The drugs entered our system through our muscles. Muscles aren't a bad way to deliver drugs because there're lots of them and they can be relatively large targets." Regan eyed Colby's biceps. "There's no muscle at that injection point. That site is used to access a vein. Veins are really hard to get into when someone is struggling."

"You're suggesting he might have been a willing participant?"

"I don't know. I'm just saying it looks weird. They could have knocked him out and then drugged him to keep him down longer. We'll have to wait until he wakes up."

Regan neared the box and began to remove its contents. Towels. Irrigation solution. A suture kit. Sutures. Sterile gauze. Antibiotic ointment. Bandages. Protein bars. Water.

Nothing fancy. No lidocaine to numb the area as was standard for stitch placement, but everything else she needed to fix Colby's laceration.

"There's no numbing medicine, but you can handle a few stitches without anesthetic, right?" Regan asked.

Colby took two steps away from her.

Regan's suggestion that he allow himself to be stitched without the area being numbed was barbaric to him. Sure, he was tough, but was he that tough? He *hated* needles. Not just a strong dislike but outright disdain. Maybe fear bordering on phobia.

"Colby. Really?" Her voice was firm and somewhat surprised. "If I don't clean and close that cut, it's going to get infected. The scarring will be much worse."

"It's going to leave a scar?"

Regan bent over and began scooping items up into her arms. "Every cut that needs stitches leaves a scar. Come on, it will be a story to tell your children one day about how you saved a woman and her daughter and..." Regan's voice trailed and she took one edge of a towel and dabbed the inner corners of her eyes. "Seriously. You're willing to take a bullet, but getting stitches has you terrified?"

"I don't like needles."

"Congratulations, you're a normal human. Now, sit yourself back in the corner and step up so we can get this done. Hopefully our additional guest will be awake by then."

Colby did as she asked. Bringing the supplies closer, she knelt next to him. "You're going to have to lie down on your left side." He settled into the position as she'd instructed and she brushed sand and dirt from his hair. Her touch caused his nerves to tingle and he couldn't help but be captured by her beauty in spite of the jeans and ragged flannel shirt she wore. She caught his gaze and he looked away, like a child trapped with his hand in the cookie jar.

"This is just saline. Rest your head on the towels. It's going to be cold."

With one hand, she held his head down and squirted the solution into the cut. He clenched his teeth as the freezing water was forced into the cut under pressure. It was all he could do to not reach up and force her hand away and maintain the image of a street-tough bounty hunter when he wanted to cry like a baby.

"Everyone always says they have a high tolerance for pain until they experience real trauma. When that happens, you see what a person is really made of," Regan said. She stopped irrigating and tore open one of the packages of sterile gauze and dried the cut, then she took a towel and mopped the rogue water drops off the rest of his face and neck.

"And what's your assessment of me?" Colby asked. His heart fired in his chest for asking. Why did he care to know her thoughts on the matter?

"Can you lie on your back? It will be easier to get the stitches in."

He rotated and settled his arms against his sides. He'd never felt so vulnerable.

Regan prepped the laceration kit next to him, opened the sutures and dropped them into the middle of the cache of metal instruments. She turned slightly away from him, opening another package of gloves, given away by the snapping rubber.

"Are you avoiding my question?" Colby asked. Blood coursed through his veins. It was a good thing he was lying down otherwise he might have just passed out. He hadn't felt this nervous since the first time he'd met his wife.

She reached into the kit and pulled out a blue towel. "Rule number one—don't touch this." She placed it on his chest. "Rule number two—don't move."

Clearly, she was needling him. Or maybe she

didn't know what to say and was preparing to let him down gently. He eyed her as she worked to place the needle in an instrument, a long tail of suturing material trailed behind it.

"Do you want the truth?" Regan asked.

Colby swallowed heavily. This was ridiculous. Why had he even started down this road? He was here for one reason: to save Sam. That was all that mattered.

"Now, you're not answering my question," she said. Was that lilt in her voice teasing?

"Of course." What else could he say? *No, I want you to lie. Tell me what every man wants to hear.*

"Hold still," she ordered.

With one hand, she pinched the skin on his forehead and in less than a breath the needle bit into his skin. His stomach turned as she pulled the thread through, and he pressed his hands into the cement.

"You're like no other man I've ever met," Regan said as her hands worked swiftly to tie a knot and trim the ends.

Colby inhaled sharply. Was it the next stitch being placed or utter surprise at her comment? Still, her words weren't necessarily a compliment. "What's been the quality of men you've met?"

Regan outright laughed and pressed her forearm against her mouth, her eyes tearing. Colby didn't know what to do so he decided to stay silent and obey rules one and two. After a few seconds, but what felt like a few hours, she lowered her arm. "You're not helping me stay sterile by saying something like that." Another stitch. Short threads from the cut line flitted onto his face.

How many was he going to need? The only good thing was that the conversation was keeping his mind off the pain.

Maybe that was her intention in dragging the conversation out.

"I have met good men before..." she started tentatively.

There was a story there. He could see it in her eyes—a level of trust that he could be the keeper of these words and not betray her emotionally.

He didn't feel the bite of the next stitch, his mind so enraptured by what she would say next.

"I thought Olivia's father was a good man." Her shoulders lowered slightly, her eyes vacant.

Colby let her be. Why press her? She would tell him what she wanted to when she was ready. Forcing her words would make him feel like a bully.

Regan turned back to him. "I think this is the last one," she said.

Before he knew it, she was done. She cleared his chest of the sterile towel and instruments and then dabbed some antibiotic ointment over the sutured cut. Grabbing a Band-Aid, she withdrew it from the package. She pressed it to his forehead and smoothed her thumbs over the edges to secure it in place.

Unknowing exactly what possessed him, he sat up and grabbed her hand. “I’d like to hear about your life. About what happened with your marriage.”

She eased away and began putting the instruments back into the empty plastic tray. “We were good in the beginning. He was everything I could have asked for. Handsome. Kind. Caring. Everything was good as long as I was inferior to him. There was an imbalance of power in our relationship. As long as I needed him more than he needed me then we were fine. At first, it seemed like I was living every girl’s dream—being so taken care of. In reality, it was a prison.” She looked up at what held them in this room. “Just without bars.”

“When did things change?”

“When I started getting media attention for some of my work, he started to get verbally abusive. It was strange. He would spend hours trolling the internet looking for articles about me and it would just set him off. I suspect he was even leaving negative comments on some of the news stories, but I could never prove it. Just a hunch.”

She looked down, and Colby placed his hand over hers. She couldn't quell the trembling that took hold. The body always physically betrayed emotion in some manner.

"Sad thing was that I was okay with the abuse as long as it didn't affect Olivia. Even when he hit me—he was always very good about injuring me in areas I didn't have to hide. Never my face, arms or lower legs."

Colby wanted to hold her but waited. He gathered her hand between both of his. "I'm sorry."

A tear fell unchallenged. "I only drew a line when he hit me once in front of Olivia. I knew then that it wouldn't be long before his anger spilled over into her territory. That eventually there would be no boundary. What hurts more is that his parents took his side. Even my parents were deluded by his charming ways. Maybe it's best, if they all feel that way, that Olivia doesn't have any contact with any of them. But it's hard—being just the two of us."

She pulled away from him and stood.

It wasn't that he didn't know what to do for Regan but that he was afraid to do it. He hadn't offered himself in an emotional way to a woman since his wife had died. After she was gone, he'd built a wall around his heart, one defiant brick at a timc. Even with Sam and his mother, he always held them at arm's length. Sometimes life was easier denying that having a deep emotional connection with someone was actually what made life worth living.

But losing it was also what made life so painful—at times unbearable.

If he put himself more than just physically on the line for Regan, what did that mean? Could they have any sort of relationship if they lived through this imprisonment? Did he want that? Was he ready?

He didn't know if he was ready, but neither could he deny that his thoughts about this mission were changing. It was becoming more about just getting them all through this alive—including Sam. It was almost as if he wanted to stay in this cell with her indefinitely because it was becoming hard for him to imagine Regan Lockhart not being part of his life.

He glanced her way. She was busying herself organizing their supplies. After that, she neared the sleeping man and shook him gently.

He opened his eyes and grabbed her.

ELEVEN

Regan yanked her hand away from Brian's grip, losing her balance and backpedaling a few steps right into Colby. He grabbed her shoulders and steadied her until she found her footing. The closeness of his body and his hands on her shoulders knotted her stomach. How could she rid herself of these reactions to Colby's presence?

Reluctantly, she eased away from Colby and sat on the floor, next to her old coworker. Brian's eyes were open, but he was in that foggy haze of his mind trying to orient his current surroundings with the memory of the last event it recorded. The more he blinked, the more frightened he appeared. He winced in pain and reached up and began to pat his head.

"Brian, do you remember me?" Regan asked.

He groaned and rubbed his forehead. "My head is killing me."

"Let me take a look," Regan said.

Colby positioned himself in her line of sight. A look of caution crossed his face.

Regan leaned forward. She didn't see any dried blood in Brian's hair. With gentle fingers, she found a large lump on the back of his head but no open wound, and the bone seemed stable underneath the injury. It didn't mean his skull wasn't fractured—just likely not in a way that would kill him.

"Doesn't look like you need stitches or anything," Regan said.

"Nice break," Colby replied, settling his shoulder against one of the bars.

Brian's pale blue eyes found hers. His longer, dark brown hair was disheveled. "Dr. Lockhart? What's going on? Where are we?"

"You do remember me."

"Is that good or bad?" Colby asked.

Why was Colby so testy all of a sudden? That would be the last time she'd ever stitch a grown man without anesthetic.

"How did you come to be here?" Regan asked.

"I was walking between my lab and my home when someone attacked me. I woke up here. What is this place?"

Footsteps echoed down the hall and the two black-clad men, currently dubbed Baldy and Green Eyes in Regan's mind, approached the cell. Baldy still grasped his automatic weapon.

Green Eyes had a holstered sidearm but held a ring of keys.

"Good. Everyone seems to be awake," Green Eyes said, inserting a key into the lock.

Baldy trained his weapon at the three of them to prevent any serious thoughts of fighting back.

Colby edged away from the cell, his fists clenched at his sides.

"The two of you—" Green Eyes pointed to Regan and Brian "—are coming with me. You, sir, will be going on a little walk with my friend here."

Regan's heart fell through the floor. "No, we stay together."

"That's not going to happen," Baldy said, testy.

Why did they want Colby by himself? A sharp pain pierced her gut. Were they going to kill him? She couldn't bear to have that happen.

Regan grabbed the cell bars with both of her hands. "If you want me to cooperate, then Colby goes where I go."

Baldy sighed as if her insistence bored him to tears. "Dr. Lockhart, *Colby* will be fine. No harm will come his way as long as he's a good little boy." He took his index finger and made an X over the left side of his chest. "Cross my heart."

The message paired with the sneer of his lip came across as a threat instead of a reassurance.

Colby laid a comforting hand on her shoulder. “It’s all right, Regan. If they wanted me dead, they would have already done it. Just go with them and see what they want.”

Regan dropped her hands from the bars. “If you don’t keep your word then I’ll do everything I can to make sure whatever your plan is fails.” She stepped back so the door could open.

“That’s big talk considering we have your daughter whose life depends on how successful you are with your tasks,” Green Eyes said.

They motioned Brian out of the cell first. Regan turned back to Colby.

He smiled at her, his blue eyes soft. “See you soon.”

She nodded and turned away, refusing to look back. It was almost as if she was splitting in two. The one thing she’d come to depend on to get her through this crisis might not be there for her when she got back.

No matter what these men say, how can I trust someone who violently takes me and my daughter as hostages and constantly threatens to do us harm?

More than that, Regan depended on Colby in a way she’d never depended on a man before. She did trust him. Trusted him to do what was in her best interest because he’d already proved he'd act on her behalf when it put him—his own life—on the line.

He was willing to sacrifice himself for her.

Men like this really existed?

Regan followed Green Eyes down the hall, looking side to side for any sign of Olivia, or even an exit. Evidently, Green Eyes didn't view either her or Brian as much of a threat considering he was allowing them to follow.

They turned right down a long cement hallway and Green Eyes unlocked the first set of doors with the keys. They then stood in front of a second set of doors that required a key code. Green Eyes shielded the lock with his hand, preventing Regan from seeing the sequence. There was a faint beep before Green Eyes pushed open the second set of doors and motioned them through before they hissed closed.

What kind of pathogens did they hold here? The sound at the doors gave it away as a negative pressure space.

The space resembled her old lab—almost an exact replica of it. The place where she'd first started her work in creating her cure for brain cancer. However, it didn't bring forth any feelings of homey reminiscence.

It was like she'd been shot with a healthy dose of anxiety.

"Look familiar?" Green Eyes asked.

Regan stepped forward and walked the span of the room. It was large. She smoothed her hand over one of the metal tables. There was no dust. The equipment looked new—high-tech microbiology equipment. There were even instruments she'd wished she had funding to buy that would make her current research easier. Regan turned in the other direction and saw the red-and-white cooler perched on the end of another table.

"Why are we here?" Brian asked.

Regan turned back to Green Eyes. A hissing sound in her ears clouded the thoughts that collided like viruses destroying healthy cells. What did they expect her to do? Could she do it?

Would she do it?

"Dr. Lockhart, early in your career there was an accident at your lab," Green Eyes said.

Statement of fact. Not a question. Regan stayed silent.

"Several workers died," he continued.

She swallowed hard. Never did a doctor want to cause death. Being a witness to its ravages was different. What did this man know?

"We want you to recreate the virus that killed them."

Regan gripped the cool metal of one of the tables with one of her hands. Her vision fuzzed briefly. Finding her dead coworkers, who'd wanted nothing more than to give others life, had been one of Regan's greatest defeats. Even though the cause of the accident hadn't been clearly delineated, she'd felt wholly responsible.

Brian reeled on his heels and faced her. "What is he talking about? It was an accident. You always said it was an accident."

"It was. I don't know what killed those people. No—not just people, my friends."

Green Eyes shook his head coolly. "That's not really true, though, is it, Dr. Lockhart?"

Regan shook her head against his words. "I don't know what killed those people."

"But you have your suspicions. Actually, I think you do know, but have never been able to admit it to yourself. That you and your work were responsible for the deaths of three people."

Brian's eyes implored hers. "Regan?"

He'd never called her that. He'd always been respectful, almost to the point of annoyance.

Regan clenched her teeth. "Why don't you just spell out exactly what you think happened and what you want me to accomplish here?"

"We believe you created a highly virulent form of airborne polio, and that when it was presumably accidentally released into the lab by one of the workers, it instantly killed all of them. We want you to replicate it. We believe the virus you're using to treat your patients has the components needed to accomplish that task, so you won't have to start from scratch, as they say. A little reverse engineering should do the trick.

"Brian is here to serve as your lab assistant. He was there at the time—interestingly, the only surviving worker on site. We're hopeful the two of you can find a way to make this happen—better sooner than later."

"You want me to create a bioweapon?"

"Dr. Lockhart, you really shouldn't concern yourself with what we plan to do with the virus."

"Creating bioweapons is against the law. International law. Even if it wasn't, it goes against everything I believe in. I won't do it."

Green Eyes placed his hand on his sidearm. "I strongly suggest you reconsider. I know you may not care about your life. The truth is sometimes being kept alive is the best torture around. I don't even have to lay a hand on you. All I have to do is torture your daughter—in front of you. Your life, the happiness or despair of the years you have left, are based on the decision you make in this moment. Will you be leaving here with your daughter alive or planning her funeral?"

And with those words, Green Eyes left her to decide.

Baldy shoved Colby out the door into a fenced-in space. He could see a guard tower with a man inside. Had this facility served as an actual prison at one point? The sun was bright and high in the sky. Midday perhaps—presumably the day after he and Regan were kidnapped. Day three of his adventure with Regan.

Colby's stomach growled. Why hadn't he first grabbed some of the food in the box? His tongue was thick from dehydration. If they were going to make it through this alive, he had to insist that Regan do more than take care of others. He at least had fat and muscle reserves to draw from. She had very little.

He strolled to the center of the yard. The ground was patchy with grass. Looking up, there was chain-link fencing strewed across the top of the squared-off space. Even prisoners weren't penned in in such a fashion.

Only animals were.

Colby continued to walk toward the fence. It appeared normal. No sign that it was electrified. He thought back to the prison cell he'd woken up in with Regan and Brian. There hadn't even been concrete slabs elevated off the ground for them to sleep on. Then he remembered the metal loops that hung from the ceiling with remnants of dangling rope.

This wasn't an old prison. Where he and Regan had been wasn't a cell designed to hold humans. These places held animals. Big ones.

That likely meant they were in some sort of lab

facility. Still operating? Sanctioned? Off grid? Unknown. The pieces of this whole mysterious undertaking were starting to form a loose picture in his mind. It made some sense why he'd seen Nico at Regan's house. Someone Colby knew who'd transitioned into military work involving managing microbes.

Now this weird facility… Colby could only imagine what would have been kept in these cages. It wouldn't be worth building something so extensive unless it was for large primates.

He walked the perimeter of the fence to do a little reconnaissance. The building was X-shaped. It looked sterile from the outside. Dark, large-brick-constructed walls and tinted windows. From another side, in a field slightly off in the distance, were numerous dog houses. What could those have been used for? To hunt and track animals? Had something nefarious escaped from this facility?

The longer he was apart from Regan the more his stomach chewed itself up. Twenty minutes had passed but it felt like hours. He'd done enough laps around the yard to have created his own little trail of worry. Baldy was as stoic as the famed British guards in front of Buckingham Palace minus the fancy outfit.

He didn't appear to want to talk, and Colby didn't engage him.

In the absence of someone else to talk to, Colby's mind wandered. How were his parents? How was Sam doing? Quickly, thoughts of Regan pushed his family out of his mind.

He reached up and touched the bandage where her hands had fixed the cut to his forehead. Having her so physically close had been unnerving. Just thoughts of her presence caused his heartbeat to stammer.

Even different from that was what he felt. Rarely had he ever felt cared for—like his needs were more important.

During Brook's treatment, if he were truthful, he'd surrendered all of himself with little in return. He didn't begrudge her that and he'd do it again. But being her primary caretaker had both given him things he didn't want to carry and taken things he desperately needed to have. Cancer had robbed him of a feeling of security. Of safety. It became the overwhelming theme of their lives: that he and Brook were victims of circumstance. What cancer had given Colby when Brook died was the sense that it wasn't worth risking a relationship with any other woman. The heartbreak was too great. He wouldn't survive something like that happening to him again.

But living in loneliness was beginning to feel worse and he was starting to think he might abandon his isolation to be with Regan—that she was worth putting his heart on the line for.

He both abhorred and loved the idea. It made him physically ill—nauseated, weak in the knees, light-headed.

Colby needed to see her; wanted to know that she was okay. The longer they were held apart, the more he wanted to rip limb-from-limb the man that stood at the door.

Colby sat and leaned against the fence. Prayer was not a usual thing in his life and he tended to only do it when his back was against the wall. When Brook had been sick, he'd prayed more than he'd ever thought possible. Feeling connected to God was still foreign to him. He mostly felt betrayed by God for unanswered prayers. For Brook still dying when he'd cried out, literally, for her life to be spared. For his to be taken instead.

He leaned his head against the fence and turned his face toward the sun, feeling it soak into his skin. Somehow it soothed his frayed nerves.

Lord, You and I haven't been on the best terms. Maybe You've been there for me and I just haven't seen it. I want to be able to see it. I want to be able to trust You. Trust that You want what's good for me. Please, help me strategize a way to get all the innocent people here out alive. Regan, Olivia, me and Brian. Help me to see what's really going on here.

Bring Regan back to me. Let her be unharmed.

His mind drifted to their last moments together. They were essentially twins now—each with matching cuts to their foreheads. It was easy to think of a woman like Regan as someone who didn't need any help...didn't want any help. She was beautiful, successful—seemingly with everything life had to offer. It just proved you couldn't judge someone's inner thoughts, feelings and emotions by how they presented themselves with clothing, housing and their job.

Emotionally, she struggled. He needed her head in the game.

For all their sakes.

Inside, Regan was broken by the betrayal of her family. By the demands of her job. And she still put her needs behind those of everyone else—her daughter, her patients and even a man relatively unknown to her. The thought of how she'd been treated by her family, her ex-husband... All that had been laid at her feet would overwhelm anybody. It made Colby angry. Yet, Regan was still standing. He could change that. Taking care of her was different because she could give something back. She'd already done so.

She had given him her trust.

The door into the courtyard opened and Regan walked through. Colby scrambled to his feet and pushed away from the fence. She ran to him and he stopped, opened his arms to her, and she fell into him, burying her face into his chest.

Her body shook from sobbing, and his heart exploded in wild fear. He gripped her tightly and pressed his lips to the top of her head. He could feel his chest vibrate in response to her distress.

He wanted to say something but as soon as he opened his mouth to proffer something reassuring, the words were broken from his own emotion.

Colby pressed his lips closed and rubbed her back.

Eventually the crying eased and he could feel her bring up a hand to wipe her tears, but she didn't pull away from him. He swallowed hard. "What is it?"

Regan sniffed. "It's terrible what they want." She pulled away and looked into his eyes, as if he were her anchor—the only thing holding them steady in the torrent winds they found themselves in.

"A bioweapon. They want me to take my cure and morph it into the deadliest bioweapon there is."

Colby's mouth dropped and he pulled her

against him because he didn't want her to interpret his muteness as distance between them.

That, despite all odds, they were in this together.

It was like his time in the military: when he had first joined, it was to avoid the emotional trauma of his wife dying. It had eventually morphed into him staying out of true duty and honor in serving his country. Delta Force missions often were one thing in the beginning and by the end the goal had changed dramatically.

When Colby first became involved with Regan, it was simply to ensure that Regan delivered the cure to Sam before she died. Now, that wasn't the case.

A switch had turned in Colby's mind. The mission had changed. An injustice was being committed against Regan. Not only had these men taken her daughter from her—the heartache and anxiety that caused any mother was profound—they'd also killed someone she'd trusted. Not only that, they'd also thrown each of Regan's patients and their families down a well of uncertainty.

Colby was sure even his own mother likely thought Regan had abandoned her patients. Had news of her stealing the virus from the public been reported in the news yet? If it had, paired with the police naming Regan as a person of interest in Polina's murder, Colby didn't think he'd ever be able to change his mother's mind from being poisoned against Regan.

An injustice was occurring. They were asking Regan to proactively develop a weapon from her cure that would be one hundred percent lethal. They were asking—no, forcing—her under coercion to actively take lives. It was against everything she believed. Her war was against death and now they were asking her to summon the Grim Reaper forth for how many lives?

The only thing that could right an injustice when words wouldn't change the situation was war.

Colby and Regan werc now comrades in a war against these men.

TWELVE

Regan and Colby were shoved back into their cell where their detention accommodations had changed. There were now three cots with sleeping bags, pillows and extra blankets. Each cot had a tray of food on the end.

Regan stepped closer to examine the offerings. Peanut butter and jelly sandwiches with potato chips and a soda. Regan's chest caved. Were they eating these things because they were Olivia's favorites? Did the hostage-takers know that? Or was it simply dinner? Something cheap and easy because it didn't require refrigeration. Regan touched the pop can. It was warm.

"We should eat," Colby said, his words funneling through her like a comforting, warm spring breeze.

Regan picked up the tray and sat on her cot. Colby grabbed his, sat and faced her. Brian walked toward them and positioned his cot so instead of being side-by-side they were triangulated—easier for a conversation.

Regan took a bite and the sandwich was as dry as a stack of stale saltine crackers. They were all likely dehydrated. Even if it was the close of just one day she and Colby hadn't had much to eat, let alone drink. She opened the pop can and took a swig. Lemon-lime bubbles effervesced in her mouth like pop rocks and after several seconds of purposeful chewing she was able to get the whole glob down.

"That good?" Colby asked.

Regan set the tray aside. Despite wanting to please Colby, and knowing his statement about eating when they could was true, she just couldn't do it. Her stomach was knotted with worry about Olivia.

"I think you two should tell me what happened," Colby said.

"What do you mean?" Regan asked.

Colby took a swig from his drink. "One of you knows what they're talking about—about what happened in that lab. It's the reason why we're all here."

Guilt clawed up Regan's throat. Her stomach turned. One of the worst times in her professional career and Colby was asking her to revisit it. To disclose what her worst fear was.

To reveal what she'd always been in denial about.

"Brian?" Colby pressed.

He shrugged. "I don't know what happened. I go home from work one day and the next, three people are dead and I've lost my job."

Regan narrowed her eyes. It seemed like such an odd thing to pair together. His words tinged bitter more at the latter part of his statement.

"One of you must have a theory. Come on, this is crazy. Spill it."

Regan's skin crawled and she clenched the metal bar of the cot. Why was this so hard to share? Because it proved she wasn't as good as she thought she was. That she'd likely made a mistake and it had cost people their lives.

Looking at Colby, she could see in his eyes that he wouldn't take anything less than what he believed to be an honest statement. But providing such information riddled her with anxiety. What would he think of her? Would he still want to be with her?

She blinked—the thought causing her mind to tilt off kilter. Is that what she wanted? To be with him? Not just now but after?

"Regan... Brian... It will be better for me if I know what we're up against. We can only plan a defense when we know the truth about what's going on. Consider this a fact-finding mission. No judgments about whatever happened, okay?"

Colby reached out to her, settled his hand on her knee and squeezed gently. "Please, trust me."

Regan pulled her lip through her teeth. Could sharing her theory really make anything worse than it really was? Of course, Colby could hate her and never want to have anything to do with her again.

"At the time I was running the lab, we were working on early versions of what became the cure I have today."

"Modifying viruses should come with some care, don't you think?" Brian asked, an edge to his voice.

He blamed her. They both could have died just as easily. But had she been careless?

"Of course. And I was careful," Regan said, defiant.

"The results say differently," Brian pressed.

Colby raised his hands. "The two of you antagonizing one another is not going to help our situation."

Regan folded her hands in her lap. "To theorize about what happened, you have to first understand what polio does in its natural state. Most people infected with polio won't even know they've contracted it. Some make it through a polio infection with mild symptoms like other viral illness—fever, sore throat and headache. However, a small minority of people suffer from the most serious complications when it attacks their nervous system, which can lead to paralysis."

"When you try and change a virus, there can be serious consequences," Brian said.

What was Brian's deal? Did he feel that she should have been punished? That she'd gotten away with something?

Regan tried not to look at Brian's intense stare. "The paralysis can affect the muscles that help a person breathe. If those muscles stop, then your body won't pull any air in."

Colby nodded. "Was there an autopsy performed on the bodies?"

"There was," Brian affirmed.

"And?" Colby said, pushing Regan to talk with the intense nature of his gaze.

"The autopsy showed that all three workers had died from suffocation."

"At the same time?" Colby asked.

"Considering the nature of how they were found, it was presumed that they died within a few minutes of each other."

"How is that possible?" Colby asked.

Regan's throat tightened into a hot and achy lump. This was the moment when everything changed.

"Polio virus can be transmitted a couple of ways, but one way is person-to-person via droplets. Someone coughs or sneezes onto a surface. You touch that surface and then touch your mouth. It's highly contagious."

"So the workers touched some active polio virus and died?" Colby asked.

Regan shook her head. "No, I don't think that's what happened."

"The evidence doesn't support that," Brian said.

"What does the evidence show?"

"Well, first you need to know what the normal incubation period is for polio—the time it takes for the disease to develop once you've been exposed—which, depending on the type of polio, can be three to twenty-one days. The issue is, those deaths couldn't have been from a previous exposure because I'd shut the lab down for a long Christmas break, which was over three weeks."

"Then?" Colby prodded.

Regan fidgeted. "On autopsy, evidence of the polio virus was found in the muscles that control respiration and nowhere else. That, along with some other signs, led to the thought that the workers had died from polio exposure—exposure to death in a matter of minutes. It's unheard of. I still don't think it's clinically possible."

Colby looked like she'd felt during a computer coding class she'd tried once—like she and Brian were discussing a foreign language. "The issue is that we know they didn't contract normal polio because of the time frame. They hadn't been to the lab in over three weeks, which is outside what we know to be the normal incubation period. The polio virus was found to be concentrated primarily in their diaphragms, the largest muscle associated with breathing. Plus, evidence of dead viral particles was also found in the ventilation system."

Colby nodded slowly. "They breathed it in."

"And it killed them within a few minutes of exposure. Nothing kills that fast."

"Nothing?"

"Nothing biological. There are a few chemical agents that kill very rapidly and most are neurotoxins."

"If there's something more effective in killing people out there, why mess with this polio virus?"

Colby verbalized what she'd been thinking a lot about over the last two days. Why pursue this as a biological weapon?

"A chemical agent puts everyone at risk, including those who deploy it. A shift in the wind can bring the agent back around, killing your own troops. However vaccines can be developed against viruses, so, in theory, you could develop a deadly biological agent and immunize your troops against it, thereby preventing their deaths even if they were exposed."

And what would the hostage-takers really do if they got what they wanted? Let her go? Doubtful. They'd need a scapegoat and a story. She could see the headline: Rogue Doctor Steals from Hospital and Disappears with Daughter—Kills Nanny With Potential Knowledge of Her Evil-Doings. Once they had what they wanted, they were all going to die.

That meant, even if she could do what they asked for, she could never give them what they wanted.

"Have they asked you to develop a vaccine, as well?" Colby asked.

"No," Regan said.

"What does that mean?" Brian asked.

"That maybe they really don't care about the consequences," Colby offered.

Regan lay down on her cot and looked up at the ceiling. Disclosing this truth had taken everything out of her, and her body, physically and mentally, was starting to spiral into a shutdown schedule. She hadn't felt this way in a long time—so spent. Not since she'd gone through divorce proceedings. How was there any way out of this? Truth was, there wasn't. How long would they give her to do as they asked? Her work had taken almost a decade to get to the point it was at now. And in truth, it wasn't like she knew exactly what had happened at the lab. When they went back to look at the polio samples, the viral samples were benign. Whatever airborne virulent strain of polio had burned itself out probably as quickly as those who had died.

"What are you going to do?" Colby asked.

Regan closed her eyes and ignored his question.

On the morning of day four they were awakened by the sound of a police baton banging on the cell bars. Colby jolted up, launched out of bed and landed on his feet with his fists raised by his face, ready for battle, before his mind reoriented him to the current state of their affairs. He turned to his right, where Regan's cot was, and she was sitting bolt upright with her covers pulled up to her chin even though she'd slept in the jeans and flannel shirt they'd been taken in. Brian had rolled out of bed and was slowly coming up off the floor with his hands raised.

This can't be good.

One thing Colby had learned from serving in the military was that it meant bad things for hostages the more men there were who brandished weapons of lethal force. Colby stood between his and Regan's cots. Two men they were familiar with—Baldy and Green Eyes as Regan called them. The third man—crew-cut blond hair and light brown eyes—Colby labeled Ice Man for the unwavering glare in his eyes. The men held nothing—no food or water. Strike that. They did hold mean, angry, condescending looks.

"Hands up!" Ice Man yelled.

Colby and Regan raised their hands. Regan looked bleary-eyed, even with the adrenaline-laced start to their morning. Not enough sleep? Checking out mentally? Giving up? None of these was good.

When Ice Man approached Regan and Colby, he took the muzzle of his gun and pressed it into Colby's chest. "Take three steps to the side."

A cool sweat broke out on Colby's forehead, belying the toughness he wanted to portray. Every instinct fired flaming-red warning flags. Physically separating him from Regan meant they were going to hurt her and didn't want him to interfere.

That wasn't going to happen.

"I said step aside!" Ice Man shoved the weapon hard into Colby's chest, causing him to take a step backward to keep his balance. Colby complied with the request. The angrier the hostage-taker became, the more brutal his retaliation would be.

Ice Man stepped directly in front of Regan. Baldy and Green Eyes held weapons trained on Colby and Brian.

Ice Man placed his face a few inches from Regan's. "You didn't give us what we asked for."

Regan inhaled deeply.

Buying time? Collecting her thoughts? Colby held his breath. What was she going to say?

"I gave you polio. That's what you asked for," Regan said.

"Tests have confirmed that you gave us *regular* polio. What did you do—raid someone's stock virus? Where is your modified virus?"

"Somewhere safe."

Ice Man leaned back and backhanded Regan across the face.

Colby's vision washed white and he launched himself into the air, one arm arcing over his head, coming down and grabbing the man around the neck, forcing Ice Man's face into the concrete.

In the next split second Baldy and Green Eyes pounced, pulling Colby off Ice Man and throwing him into the cell bars. Ice Man scrambled to his feet, patting the floor for his sidearm that had been knocked loose during the tackle. Baldy and Green Eyes grabbed Colby, one at each arm, and held him tight against the bars.

Ice Man pawed at his nose with the back of his hand and wiped the blood away. His chest heaved. "No food or water for little Olivia today."

Colby leaned his head against the bars. He couldn't bear to look at Regan's face, knowing his actions to protect her were going to cause her daughter harm. This dynamic he and Regan were in was constantly changing. Every move on the chessboard convinced Colby that these weren't some two-bit criminals hoping to score a virus.

They were seasoned military men bent on obtaining a weapon of mass destruction. If Colby's assumption were true, then keeping all the hostages alive meant little to them. They were all merely to be used as leverage against one other.

Regan neared Ice Man. Her eyes narrowed. "Having the modified polio virus won't help us here. Whatever happened in my old lab was generations before that cure was developed. If you want me to try and replicate the work I did in that lab, then you have to let me go get my old journals."

Ice Man stepped away from her, a small stream of blood still trickling from his nose. He threw his hands up in the air. "What kind of fool do you take me for? How hard can this be? You've done it once—you can do it again."

"It not that easy and it's more likely than not that I won't be able to replicate what happened even with my notes. Sometimes we don't always understand what happens in a petri dish. Science is not so clear-cut and experimental results can't always be repeated."

The man clenched his teeth. "Where. Are. These. Notes."

"In a safe-deposit box at a bank close to where I live."

The man paced in a circle, weighing the decision in his mind. In these moments Colby wished he knew the inner workings of Regan's mind better. Did these notes exist? And if they did, did she actually need them for her work? Or was this a ruse? Was she developing some elaborate escape plan in her mind?

"Fine. We'll take you to this bank."

"You'll need to take me back to my house so that I can get the key," Regan said.

"That's not going to happen. You'll tell us where the key is and we'll secure it by other means."

"Fine." Regan crossed her arms over her chest. "The sooner we go, the sooner I can get started."

The men's arms grew tired of holding Colby and they lessened the pressure pinning him against the bars.

Ice Man, still zeroed in on Regan, sniffed hard. "This is how this is going to work. Olivia will stay here under our gentle, loving care. If you don't return with these notes from the bank, we're killing the three of you, packing everything up and leaving Olivia here to die scared and alone from starvation."

Regan nodded. "Understood."

"We take you and your friend." Ice Man nodded Colby's direction. "He seems emotionally invested in your well-being. If either of you make an attempt to escape while we're on our little field trip then it will be one bullet in the other person's head. Is that understood?"

Regan kept her gaze steady. "It is."

"Then we seem to have reached an agreement."

Ice Man waved his hand and all three men vacated the cell, the door clanging like a sharp nail down Colby's spine. He walked to Regan who'd plopped herself back on her cot. The imprint of the attacker's hand remained red against her cheek.

He sat next to her, and she leaned against him. "I don't blame you for what's going to happen to Olivia."

Colby's throat ached. There had to be something that he could do. In the military he'd never been at anyone else's mercy. It was a position he didn't like to be subjugated to. "I just couldn't stand to see anyone hurt you. I should have stayed put. I just…couldn't."

Regan rested her hand on his leg, and he pulled her closer with his hand on her shoulder. If he and Regan weren't locked in a cage and her daughter under threat of death, there was a lot that could feel right about this moment. The two of them together—one against the world and all its craziness.

Maybe there would be a time like that for them. When this was all over. Right now, it was hard to see a time past this situation. If a time like that ever came, would she need him after this? Want him after this? Because a shift was happening in his heart. A physical movement he hadn't felt in a long time. And he was finding it hard to think of life without her in it.

Brian took a few steps and stood in front of them. "Do these journals exist? Or was this a play to just get out of here?"

"They exist. And they contain the information I said they do."

"Good. All you need to do is hold up your end of the bargain and we can all get out of here."

Bargain? Colby narrowed his eyes. Was Brian truly a hostage?

Or was he a mole?

Regan felt the gun between her shoulder blades shove her forward through the door into the yard. Of course, there were everyone's theories about prison and what it felt like to lose freedom and then there was actually living it. People could theorize ad nauseam about what something felt like, but until it was lived through, experienced fully in the flesh, then all they were merely doing was offering sympathy.

She crossed the yard to a patch of sun near the fence line and sat. Colby followed, taking a seat next to her on the grass.

It was the first time the two of them had been alone outside together. Their guard seemed disinterested in their conversation—maintaining his distance by keeping his watch at the door.

There was so much to talk about, but where to start?

"How's your face?" Colby asked.

Regan rubbed the remnants of the slap with light fingers. The skin was sore, raw. A feeling she thought she'd never have to revisit again once her ex-husband was out of her life. "Nothing that won't heal. Probably won't even leave a mark."

At least not physically.

"Tell me about Brian."

Colby's words were definitive. Not a question, but an assumption that she knew a lot when really Brian was a mystery to her. She'd even say she heard a tinge of jealousy marking those words. "What do you want to know?"

"Everything."

"Why?"

Colby raked his fingers through the sparse grass. "I think he's with them…not with us. Or not a prisoner like we are."

Regan's eyes widened slightly, but then she nodded. What Colby said was a reasonable deduction and she'd had her own suspicions, as well. The needle mark and his injuries seemed contrived. Not that they weren't real—just conveniently placed. Why was he never in the yard with them? The confrontation this morning hadn't seemed to surprise him much, and he wasn't targeted like Colby was. Did they not think he'd defend Regan just as much as Colby? If he wasn't with the hostage-takers, then why hadn't they made him take three steps to the side? Or have more men available to physically restrain him, as well, should he become unhinged? Who else could run the scientific tests to confirm the polio she'd given them wasn't her cure if not Brian?

"I get why you think that, but it also would be hard for me to believe."

"An enemy doesn't have to be big and brawny to be a threat. Sometimes the skinny, smart ones can be the biggest danger around." He turned, caught her gaze and winked.

Regan laughed. Heat flamed her cheeks and she hoped the redness wasn't visible in the light. How could she laugh, considering their circumstances? Regardless, it felt good. A lightness spread through her that she hadn't felt in a long time. Laughing with a man was something she hadn't done in a long time. Did he really mean her with his statement? A gentle teasing? And who was she a danger to? His state of mind?

Whatever it was he'd meant, it felt good—natural, despite their circumstances. And if something could feel so normal under duress, what would it be like when this stress didn't exist? What would a carefree relationship feel like with Colby?

Regan placed her elbows on her thighs. "Brian was a doctoral candidate for microbiology when I first met him. He was extremely smart. Smarter than me, probably."

"That's pretty smart."

She nudged Colby with her shoulder. "Stop it. I can't tell if you're being serious or joking."

"Isn't the fun in the mystery?"

"We have enough mystery, wouldn't you say?" Regan asked.

Colby nodded. "Agreed." His voice lowered. "We need to be serious about this, but it does feel good to laugh a bit. You're really giving our kidnappers some grief and they don't like it very much."

"No, I'm not."

"Hello. Should we discuss the drop-off and you disobeying every order they gave you *and* every instruction I gave you? You could lead a master-level class on how to aggravate your hostage-taker 101."

"Fine, I'll give you that." Something clicked in Regan's mind. "You know, that's what unnerved me about Brian when we worked together."

"What do you mean?"

"He was always… I don't know…pushing the limits, but not in a good way. A safe way."

"Like you do?" His words were sincere. She smiled.

"I mean ethical boundaries. Obviously it's true I was manipulating a virus to do and be something it wasn't designed to do, but Brian was interested in mixing things together that had potential, on paper, to be extremely lethal."

"Which leads me to believe he's not the hostage they're trying to convince us he is. What happened to Brian after the accident?"

"I know it was hard for him to find another job. Maybe that's why he has his own lab on his property."

"Why was it hard for him to find work?"

Regan leaned her head against the fence. Why did her past have to feel so tainted? There were few things she could look back on and celebrate. Her marriage had been a disaster. Her first ventures into her work had likely been responsible for the deaths of three people. Now everyone involved with her was suffering. Innocent people like Colby.

Lord, remind me of the blessings. For Olivia. For Colby. For the work I can do against cancer that will save lives.

"I didn't write Brian any letters of recommendation," Regan said.

"For the reasons you mentioned. You thought he would go on and do dangerous work?"

"For lots of reasons. He wasn't good at working for someone—or maybe he didn't like working for a woman. I don't know. He was constantly defiant. Tried to rework my protocols without my permission. He'd run his own experiments on the side to try and outpace me. Maybe prove he could get to the desired end before me. In science, it's good to have a certain amount of bravado. Particularly being a woman in this field, but you also need some humility because I've been wrong more than I've been right on the road to this cure. And if you can't learn from failure then you shouldn't do this work."

"And that's what you would say about Brian? He lacked humility? Couldn't learn from failure?"

"I'm saying that not only did he want to cross over many ethical lines, but he couldn't see the consequences of doing so. They didn't matter to him."

Regan swallowed hard. Not only were they caged, but her thoughts were beginning to align with Colby's. They were caged without defenses with a lion. And that lion wasn't the hostage-takers who wielded the weapons—it was Brian.

Had to be.

"You're not telling me anything I haven't thought already. I think we act like he's one of us. We still take care of him. Look out for his interests, but know as soon as we turn around that he's sharpening his sword behind us," Colby said.

"Which means we need our own game plan."

Regan scanned the side of the structure. If only they had more access to the building. It looked to be three stories high. Most of the windows were closed and covered.

All except one.

Regan narrowed her eyes. Was she seeing what she thought? She nudged Colby's shoulder, not wanting to point to draw the guard's attention.

"Do you see it?" she asked. "Fluttering outside the building?"

Colby shielded his eyes from the sun. "A scarf. Pink?"

Tears flowed down Regan's face. "Yes. It's Olivia's. A gift from me on her last birthday."

"A signal?" Colby asked.

Whatever it was, it was proof Olivia had been

there at some point and was hopefully still there, relatively safe and sound.

Hope spread through Regan's chest. Just getting an indication that Olivia was there was relief. The hostage-takers had every reason to keep Olivia alive if they continued to want Regan to cooperate. What would be the benefit of lying about it?

Lord, keep my daughter safe. Help Colby and me figure a way out of this that doesn't put our lives at risk. Help us to find a way.

Colby seemed to sense her thoughts. "We're two smart people. We have all the skills we need to come out of this alive. We just need to find the right path."

That was the trouble with paths. They could be straight and well-lit, but they could also be narrow, winding and dark.

Thus far, they seemed to be walking the treacherous route.

THIRTEEN

It was morning—day five of Regan's relentless nightmare. She stood in front of the mirror and looked at the image in front of her. The hostage-takers had trolled through her house to get everything she'd needed.

On the counter in front of her were her hair dryer, hairbrush and makeup case. Behind her on a rack were several outfits to pick from. What was strange was the combination they had picked. The three outfits were all ones she'd worn to press conferences about her cure. Did they not want to make a mistake in putting something together that she would never wear? Something that didn't look like her? Or had they been stalking her over these last six months and that was what had drawn their eye because it was familiar from watching those press conference tapes over and over in an effort to learn everything about her?

The clothes of her trade felt foreign to her.

Pressed pants. Silk shirts. She fingered the empty space where her stethoscope usually fell. Having something stripped away and then given back felt strange.

Baldy and Green Eyes had come into their cell early that morning and insisted that she and Colby take showers. She'd guessed it would give them away to look too disheveled getting into her bank box. The door to the bathroom locked, which provided her comfort even though Baldy remained outside. Oftentimes, she was given only a few minutes in the bathroom and she'd not been allowed to lock the door. This time she was given thirty minutes to shower, dress and look presentable.

The first few minutes of solitude she'd spent crying because she'd found one of Olivia's hair clips. One she'd bought at a specialty store because Olivia loved penguins. Regan had given it to her at Christmastime last year, and even though the hair accoutrement was out of season she'd still wanted to wear it every day.

Another bit of proof that Olivia was indeed here.

The next few minutes Regan spent looking for an escape route, but the window's bars were secure. Nothing she found could work the screws open. Why was she wasting time when they were driving out of here and a new, better opportunity might present itself?

Regan slipped on a pair of high heels and felt wobbly as she turned and opened the door. Baldy marched her out to the front of the complex where Colby stood next to the car, Green Eyes watching him.

Her breath seized in her chest. He looked different from any time she'd met him before. Gone were the faded jeans and polo shirt, replaced with a pair of gray khakis and a button-up, long-sleeved shirt that brightened the color of his sapphire-blue eyes. His face was cleanly shaved and even from a distance she caught a hint of his cologne.

A smile crested his face and he shifted shyly on his feet.

Baldy nudged her forward and positioned her beside Colby.

"I don't know where they found these clothes. I thought I'd hidden them a while back. I don't usually like to get dressed up like this," Colby said.

"Put your hands in front of your bodies," Baldy ordered.

Regan and Colby thrust their hands forward where they were zip-tied together. "I guess we can't look like vagrants when we go into the bank."

Green Eyes opened the back passenger door.

Colby got in first and shimmied across the rough, fractured leather seat to the other side. Regan sat and then pulled her legs inside.

Baldy and Green Eyes got in. Baldy, in the driver's seat, turned and smirked at Regan. "Good to see that our little altercation yesterday hasn't left any marks. Wouldn't want to draw any undo attention."

Regan hated the reminder. "How do you think this is going to work? Don't you think I'll be recognized at the bank? My picture's been all over the news."

"We'll see. People aren't as observant as you want them to be." He motioned to Green Eyes. "Sorry about this but we'll need to make sure you don't see where you're going."

Green Eyes turned in his seat with two black felt bags. People really used these things? Regan bent forward and allowed the hood to be draped over her head. Wouldn't other drivers see them like this? Wouldn't it draw suspicion?

Once their hoods were in place the car started to move. Regan's hands were folded in her lap. No seat belt in place. Losing her sight made it difficult to anticipate the bumps in the road, and she and Colby were constantly colliding into one another. Regan decided the best choice would be just to lean against him for stability.

Unknown minutes and miles passed. There

was nothing she could use to mark their time on the road so she began to count to sixty, but gave up after about twenty minutes out of boredom. The jarring of the car suggested dirt roads and it seemed like more than an hour passed before they hit smooth pavement. Shortly after that, the car jolted to a stop and the hoods came off their heads.

Regan blinked as she adjusted to the sun's glare. They were on a paved road on a hill and she could see the city below her. No cars whizzed by and she didn't see any traffic signs.

Green Eyes got out and opened Regan's door. "Get out."

She did as she was instructed. Never again would she judge a victim's decision making because until confronted with being taken hostage, no one could anticipate what they would do.

There she stood, out in the open. Green Eyes got in the car and seated himself next to Colby. Regan gazed at the open field, but quickly discarded running away. How far would she get running in high heels with her hands tied together? She returned to her seat. Green Eyes reached across her lap and pulled the car door closed. His position between the two of them offered more control.

"Keep those hands down and we won't have

any problems," Green Eyes said. He raised his weapon and flashed it before them. "Understood?"

Regan's hands slicked with sweat. She wasn't familiar with this particular road and nothing seemed recognizable. The car began to move, pick up speed, but Baldy seemed to be keeping it right around the speed limit to not draw undue attention.

They started to flow into a stream of cars. A few turns and Regan identified some landmarks and knew exactly where they were. Perhaps another ten minutes and they'd be at her bank.

Regan glanced at Colby and his eyes mirrored the concern in her own. Every nerve in her body tingled. What would happen during this exchange? Would someone recognize her immediately? Call the police? And if that happened, what next?

Baldy parked the car in the bank's lot. Green Eyes clipped the zip-ties from their wrists. Regan rubbed her skin and tried to catch Colby's gaze, but he was looking past her out the window.

To the parked police car across the street.

"Don't get any ideas," Baldy warned. "We're just here for those journals. Both of you need to remember what's at stake here. Even if the two of you make it away from here and we're arrested by the police, I can guarantee you we won't stay in jail and Olivia will die."

Regan wiped her palms on her pants.

Baldy got out of the car and opened the door for her. She stood, and he grabbed her elbow, running his hand down her arm until he reached her hand and pressed the metal key to her safe-deposit box into her palm.

His touch was the equivalent of nails on a chalkboard.

Baldy leaned forward, his lips close to her ear. His breath hot and fetid against her cheek. "If we don't check in in the next twenty minutes, they'll kill your daughter." He backed away and kissed her cheek lightly. Her stomach roiled and she bit her lip to keep from vomiting. He smiled. "So be a good little mama, okay?"

Regan nodded and pivoted on shaky feet toward the bank's entrance. She and Baldy walked close together, though he didn't keep his hands on her. Regan didn't dare look in the direction of the cop car and hoped Colby was behaving himself as he and Green Eyes walked behind them. This wasn't the time to try something daring—not with Olivia's life having a twenty-minute timer over it.

Baldy opened the door for Regan and she broached the inner sanctum of the bank. He steered her to a desk where a woman typed busily at her computer. One elderly man stood at the counter, chatting it up with a younger male clerk. Baldy nudged her forward and she nearly tipped over the leather chair in front of the woman's desk. The woman looked up, her lips downturned in annoyance until she saw Regan's face.

And then her mouth dropped open.

"Dr. Lockhart."

Strange for sure. She'd never met this woman. Her glitzy, bronze name tag read Gloria. Was this woman recognizing her good or bad?

"I need to get into my safe-deposit box," Regan said.

"Yes, of course. Do you have your key?" Gloria stood from her desk. Her hands were visibly shaking. Regan looked around the bank. Where had the elderly man gone? The clerk at the counter stood there stock-still, eyeing the foursome with a wariness of a patient who was about to go in for surgery with a fifty-fifty chance of survival.

Something was off that Regan couldn't quite put her finger on. She looked at the two televisions mounted in the corners of the lobby. Both were off when they'd normally broadcasted a 24/7 news channel every other time she'd been in the bank.

Regan lifted her chin. "Yes, right here."

"Dr. Lockhart—only one person can accompany you inside the vault. Two of your other friends will have to stay out here."

"That won't work for us," Baldy said.

Gloria looked like she might whither. Her eyes darted around and she nodded subtly—like she was responding to something someone had said to her. Was she wearing an earpiece? Regan couldn't see anything visible.

"I'm sorry, sir, but it is bank policy and something we don't waver on. I'm sorry to not be able to meet your expectations."

It was Gloria's voice—dropped a tone and soft-spoken—like Baldy was a toddler about to erupt into a tantrum.

Was this simply Gloria's training kicking in as she often dealt with testy people on financial matters? Or had Gloria been expecting them?

"Fine—"

Regan reached behind her and latched onto Colby's arm. "This gentleman will be going in with me. The items in the deposit box are private documents that are meant for him."

Baldy pushed his hand out from his jacket, glared at his wristwatch and tapped it three times. "Don't keep us waiting too long. You know we have an appointment in fifteen minutes. We can't keep them waiting without serious penalty."

Gloria stepped away from her desk. "You two gentlemen are more than welcome to take a seat here and wait. Would you like a bottled water?"

"No, but thanks for asking." Green Eyes and

Baldy pulled the chairs out from Gloria's desk and sat.

Gloria motioned Regan and Colby forward. They walked through the lobby, down a few halls and turned to a door that had a keyed access. The woman led the way. Once inside, she grabbed another set of keys and motioned them forward.

Why hadn't she asked for some sort of identification from Regan?

When they turned the corner into the vault—two men stood there. Both were dressed in military uniforms. One stood with an assault rifle strapped across his chest. The other stood calmly, his hands folded in front of him, the left chest decorated with numerous ribbons and medals.

The man appeared bald under his cap. His eyes were dark brown and narrowed as he scanned Regan and Colby as quickly and informatively as a CT scanner does a patient.

"Dr. Lockhart, I'm Nicholas Abrams. I work with the military in a position where I hunt down people operating outside the law in regard to biological agents. We've been anticipating your arrival. Seems that you've gotten yourself and Mr. Waterson into quite the situation. We're here to help."

Colby didn't know whether he should cry out with relief or punch Nicholas Abrams in the face.

He consciously flared out his fingers from both hands to prevent them from forming fists.

"Didn't ever think we'd meet again like this, Colby," Nico said.

It was unusual for men who had served so closely as part of Delta Force to be at odds. The military normally formed bonds that could never be broken.

But the one thing that could break them was being negligent to the point that someone died. Colby and Nico each held the other responsible for Mark's death, and the waters remained turbulent between them. It had been years since they'd talked.

"I'd heard you weren't serving with Delta Force anymore. Is it an agency that has a name, or are you doing covert ops and hitting United States' citizens on US soil, but no one gets to review or know anything about it?"

Regan shifted beside Colby. How could Abrams diffuse years worth of tensions between the two of them in a few short minutes? Simply, he couldn't.

"Dr. Lockhart stole a biological agent from a hospital. You think we should just let that go?"

"Depends on who *we* are and *who* you're working for."

Regan stepped forward. "Gentlemen, I hate to cut short your obviously heartfelt reunion, but my daughter's life is on the line and we don't have a lot of time to be chatting about the past."

Colby stretched his neck and dropped his shoulders to try to ease his knotted muscles. Of all the people in the world who might be able to provide assistance—why did it have to be Nico? There was little trust between them.

"To answer your question, Colby, I work for the Department of Defense. After our time in Iraq, I transitioned to their team. As you know, there has been little restraint of some foreign governments to use chemical and biological agents on non-military personnel, so my team and I try to thwart the development of these weapons. We got a call from someone trying to sell what they termed to be a virulent form of airborne polio."

"Someone called the DoD and tried to sell you a bioweapon?" Colby asked.

"You know international law strictly prohibits the formation of these weapons. And just because we weren't interested in purchasing such an agent doesn't mean that someone else wouldn't be. That's when my team got the call to investigate."

"Were you able to find out who made the call?" Regan asked.

"Yes, a man by the name of Brian Hollis."

"I knew it," Colby said.

"We started to research Brian's past and discovered the lab accident that occurred when he worked with Dr. Lockhart. What happened regarding the accident wasn't publically disclosed, but what was known was that Regan had been working with the polio virus. I became involved in Regan's case when the hospital reported her theft of her modified polio virus. It wasn't hard to start to tie these two events together." Nico turned to Regan. "And why did you steal your cure?"

"Because they're holding my daughter hostage and asked for it in exchange, but then they took me and Colby. They want me to reverse engineer the cure into a bioweapon."

Nico nodded. "Considering Brian was trying to sell something along those lines, we assumed he had some inside knowledge about what might have happened at your lab." Nico turned to Regan and asked, "Does he?"

"I don't know what Brian thinks he knows. I'm not even entirely sure what happened myself to have caused those deaths, but it appeared that the workers were killed by aerosolized polio virus. However, I don't know what happened in the lab to create it. It seemingly burned itself out."

"What did you think when Dr. Lockhart popped up missing?" Colby asked Nico.

"Were you following me?" Regan asked. "And

if you were, did you see Olivia and Polina get taken and do nothing about it?"

Regan was nearly screaming by the end of the sentence. Tears formed in her eyes and Colby wondered if her voice had carried to the lobby and alerted the hostage-takers that more was going on in the vault than her and Colby picking up a few notebooks.

"No, we didn't have you or your family under surveillance," Nico said. "We did a preliminary background check on you, but didn't find anything concerning, so we began to work other angles. It was only after you stole the virus from the hospital that we thought you and Brian might be working together. That's when we came to your house."

"I'm not working with him," Regan said. "I'm innocent. If we're not out of this vault in the next few minutes they're going to kill her."

"Regan, calm down," Colby said. None of this arguing was getting them anywhere. To Nico he said, "Just tell us what you know."

"We were able to trace the call to the DoD to a phone registered to Brian. I'd have to say, he's not a very savvy criminal, so we weren't too worried about him personally. We made him an offer—not to really purchase it but to flush him out. He didn't like it, so we guessed he'd start looking for other buyers who were willing to pay a higher price."

"Who did he find?"

"That's classified, but let's just say the person Brian found, for now, is a very bad actor. He's more or less a broker for other entities. He's looking to sell your bioweapon to the highest bidder, but they have to have a product first. If Brian has threatened you, then I would believe every word he says. Brian's life is on the line, as well, and he knows it. This broker has quite a trail of dead bodies in his wake and he's also been known to try to cut out other middle men."

Colby ran his fingers through his hair. "What's the plan? You're obviously not here to rescue us, otherwise you would have already."

"What we want to learn is who all the interested parties are. The men who have you are the low-hanging fruit. We need the top players. That's very valuable information for the US military—who is interested in buying weapons like this, what kind of money they're willing to pay and what kind of biological agents they might already have access to."

"You want me to be your spy? I'm a doctor. I don't do covert ops. I only want my daughter back safely."

"Dr. Lockhart, perhaps you don't realize how much trouble you're in. If you get me this information, it could be the only way to keep from going to jail. To get your life back." He paused and narrowed his eyes. "Can you do what Brian asks?" Nico asked. "Create a bioweapon from polio?"

Regan's head swam. That was the deal. Valuable information in exchange for immunity. "The problem is, I don't know how it was created in the lab. I know our hostage-takers are not going to wait around for me to figure it out."

Nico stepped forward and held his hand out. There were two clear gel caps in his hand. Inside each was what appeared to be a black dot. "These are locater chips. You need to swallow them."

"You're kidding, right?" Regan asked.

"Actually, no. If you have smart hostage-takers, then they'll search your clothing when you return to their location. Hopefully they won't scan you with any devices that could pick these up."

"Why don't you just follow us?" Colby asked, refusing to take one of the clear capsules from Abrams's hand. "End this thing."

"Too dangerous right now," Nico said. "When we found out there was the existence of this safety-deposit box, we've been camped out here in the basement for days to see if Regan would show up, as we have with other known associates and places. But yesterday, persons likely associated with the broker were all around this premises and even placed one inside the bank—a temp who showed up for work today in place of someone else. Some are likely still outside."

"Is the person the temp was covering for okay?" Regan asked.

"Unknown at this time, and we had someone from the bank discharge the temp. It didn't seem to raise any eyebrows," Abrams said. "Regan, we need you to find out who the other interested buyers are. This broker isn't likely the only one. You have forty-eight hours to determine that. The more information we have, the more likely we can stop your knowledge from falling into the wrong hands."

Regan took one of the pills from his open palm and eyed it warily.

"It's all right," Colby said. "Nico and I have our differences, but I've never known him to be a liar." Colby grabbed the other gel capsule and one of the water bottles sitting on the table. Taking a swig of water, he then swallowed his capsule.

This is insanity. This whole scenario is straight out of some spy movie and I'm caught right in the middle of it. A doctor. A healer. A mother.

Regan's hand started to shake. She watched Colby for a good minute. If it were poison, particularly cyanide, the signs would present themselves quickly.

"Why do I have to swallow one?" Regan asked. "Why can't you just track Colby?"

"Double insurance."

"Nico thinks the hostage-takers view me as expendable," Colby said.

Abrams smoothed his tongue over his lower teeth. "Colby's right. You're the high-value target. I'm actually surprised they've let Colby live this long. He's a physical threat to them. Only reason to keep him alive is for leverage over you. They think that you care for him. That they might be able to bend your will to theirs if they threaten his life."

That you care for him.

Are my feelings more transparent to other people than they are to myself? Do the hostage-takers sense that I'd do everything I could to protect Colby as much as Olivia?

Regan closed her eyes. They needed to get out of this vault. Time was ticking. They only had a few minutes left.

Lord, don't let taking this capsule be the death of me. Let these people be true to their word—that they're really here to help us and not harm us.

Before she could think of myriad reasons to not go along with this plan, she put the pill in her mouth, grabbed Colby's water bottle and drank it down.

"Good," Abrams said. "We'll determine your location from the chips. Colby, 1200 in two days, we'll take the compound via assault. Do whatever you can on the inside to get all the hostages in a safe place. It might be best to keep Brian alive for interrogation."

Regan showed her key. "I still need the contents of the box or they're not going to believe anything I've said I'd do."

"Of course."

Nico and his charge stepped aside. Regan and the bank woman stepped up to Box 114 and slipped their keys in. Regan pulled open the box, took out the inner core and set it on the table. She couldn't keep her mind off the capsule in her stomach. Each minute that passed she worried about it less because Colby remained upright and didn't exhibit any signs of discomfort. Anxious tendrils wormed their way through her gut. She opened the box and stared at the notebooks that contained the ghosts of her past. Black-and-white composition books. She pulled them out and the bank rep put the core back into the box.

Nico turned to Colby. "Forty-eight hours."

"Yes, sir."

They left the vault with just the bank employee and crested the stairs. Baldy and Green Eyes were pacing the center of the bank like feral cats looking for rodents. When Regan approached them, Baldy said, "You didn't have a lot of time left. What took so long?"

"My apologies, sir," Gloria said. "There was some trouble with my key. It's been happening on and off lately."

Regan exhaled slowly in relief as Gloria's answer seemed to satisfy Baldy.

The foursome walked to the car without being stopped. Regan scanned the area. There were several people milling around the bank. None seemed to give her a glance.

But who was enemy or friend? Who was with the hostage-takers? Who was against them? Did this broker still have men outside the bank? Was it even worth the time to figure it out?

Once inside the car Green Eyes took the notebooks from Regan. "Get buckled up."

As Regan pulled the strap across her chest, she saw something whistle across the parking lot.

A flash of white, pain and then blackness.

FOURTEEN

Colby's ears were ringing. Acrid smoke hung heavy in his nostrils, and his first deep breath caused a racking cough that sent spindles of sharp pain through his ribs. Everything felt off. He opened his eyes and he was back in Iraq. Smoke swirled near the bank building, and it was hard to tell if the structure had been hit or not. He was upside down—the force of the blast had taken the parked car and upended it. His seat belt dug into his abdomen. There was a pool of blood trickling from the end of his fingertips.

His mind was in a fugue state between his past and present. He groped his chest and was met by buttons and fabric versus the hard contour of his Kevlar vest and the military radio he wore when he served.

Thoughts popped like rocket fire in his mind.

Where am I? The bank. What was I doing here? With someone. Regan. Regan!

Turning left, he blinked several times and didn't see her seated next to him. He looked down and found her crumpled against the roof of the car, showered in glass, still and unmoving. He looked forward and didn't see either Baldy or Green Eyes.

Colby wasn't sure of the best way to get out of the predicament without falling right on top of Regan, but his mind hastened action. He gripped the side of the blown-out window, released the seat belt and lowered himself next to her.

Placing a hand on her back, he checked to see if she was breathing. After what felt like minutes, he finally felt a shallow rise. He couldn't see any obvious injuries, but explosions were funny things. Just the concussive force of a blast could kill a person without leaving a mark.

Colby had to get Regan out of the car. And then what? What had exploded? Who had set off the blast? Abrams's crew? Cohorts of Green Eyes and Baldy? Bad guys they didn't know? Colby settled on his knees next to Regan's head and eased her onto her back. She was limp. Unresponsive. There was a shard of glass embedded in her right arm. He resisted the urge to pull it out.

It seemed easy enough to pull her from the

car through the blown-out passenger window. He scooped his hands under her shoulders and began to crawl backward when he felt the muzzle of a gun directly behind his right ear.

"Where do you think you're going?" Baldy. The more vicious one. Alive and seemingly unharmed.

Colby glanced over his shoulder and glared. "I'm trying to get Regan out of the car. Do you have a plan?"

"There is another vehicle waiting for us. Go ahead and pull her out and then you're going to cross the street, away from the bank, to the white SUV with the hatch open across the road."

Colby shimmied and pulled Regan out. The space next to them in the parking lot was vacant, which gave Colby plenty of room to wiggle out and pull her to a flat surface. He must not have been out long. People walked around in a daze. A woman screamed in the distance. No sound of sirens.

"Pick her up," Baldy ordered. "Let's get moving."

"Do you have the notebooks?" Colby asked.

Baldy looked at him, at first perplexed, and then seemingly realizing what Colby was asking.

"Don't do anything you'll regret. Little Olivia's life is still on the line."

Baldy bent and crawled inside the front end of

the vehicle. When he emerged he had the notebooks with him. One was significantly torn and tattered around the edges, having taken the brunt of the glass breaking as the shards were propelled into the inner compartment of the car.

"Let's go," Baldy said.

The ringing in Colby's ears wasn't lessening and he found himself relying on reading lips. He scooped Regan up and dropped her over his shoulder, easing her gently into the tailback. Ice Man, armed, as well, closed the hatchback and raced to the driver's seat. Colby jumped in the back. There wasn't any way he would let them have Regan alone. Whatever happened, they'd have to take him along.

Or kill him.

Baldy got into the passenger's seat, showing Colby his gun to reaffirm the continued threat.

Colby raised his hands in surrender. While Ice Man pulled into traffic, Baldy held up a zip-tie and motioned Colby's hands forward. Colby reached his arms out and felt the plastic strap enclose his wrists. He then settled his hands in his lap and stared straight ahead. The sound from a multitude of sirens barely penetrated when the flood of emergency vehicles moved toward the bank. A divided street meant Ice Man didn't have to stop and pull over. Before much time had passed, they were outside the city limits.

The car was quiet, unnervingly so.

Colby glanced into the back. Regan remained unconscious.

"We need to take her to a hospital," Colby said.

"She'll be fine. Just knocked out. Like you," Baldy said.

"What about your friend?" Colby asked, referring to Green Eyes.

"Not knocked out. Shard of glass in the neck. Bled out, I'm sure. Or is bleeding out."

What if Green Eyes lived? Didn't Baldy worry about the man talking?

"Was that your team? Did you cause the explosion?" Colby asked.

Baldy didn't respond, seemingly lost in his thoughts. If it wasn't people friendly to their current hostage-takers, then Ice Man and Baldy had expected trouble in some measure by having a backup vehicle ready to go. Almost like the Secret Service.

"It wasn't us. The man we've been working with doesn't like middle men," Baldy finally said.

Just as Nico had said and their hostage-takers had seemingly anticipated. Had this broker tried to capture Regan directly? In such a deadly way? A way that could have easily killed her?

The driver hit a dirt road and stopped. Baldy

put the black hood over Colby's head again. "Lie down on the seat."

Colby did as instructed. At least they hadn't ordered him out of the car. He agreed with Abrams's assessment. His life was more at risk than Regan's. He was the expendable one.

Lord, please be with Regan. Let her be okay. Bring her back to me. Let her wake up. Keep Olivia and Sam safe. Help me figure out a way to end this with all of us alive and the cure intact.

Colby must have drifted off as he'd prayed because an abrupt stop and car doors slamming brought him back to the present. The hood was yanked off unceremoniously and Colby blinked against the sun. Baldy clipped the zip-tie while Ice Man watched Colby at gunpoint. Colby exited the vehicle.

The two men rounded the back of the car and opened the hatchback where Regan remained. They motioned to him and he picked her up and carried her inside.

Instead of going back to the cell, they took him to a different area of the compound. They unlocked the door and there were four medical beds with monitoring equipment.

"Do what you can for her," Ice man seethed. "For your sake, you better get her to wake up."

Colby rested her on one of the gurneys. His medical knowledge didn't near hers, but he had gone through basic EMT training for situations just like this, providing enough medical care to keep someone alive until they could be evacuated to a field hospital.

What did he do when the patient was the doctor and had all the information he needed to save her life?

Colby turned the heart monitor on and grabbed the white skin patches and placed them on her chest. Next, the blood pressure cuff. The oxygen probe on her finger. He found a stethoscope in a drawer and listened to her breathing. Everything checked out. Her heartbeat was strong, steady and not elevated. She was getting enough oxygen by just breathing room air. Blood pressure mildly on the low side of normal.

Carefully, Colby pulled Regan's eyelids up. The pupils were equal, mid-size and responding to light.

Looking at her right arm, he noticed the glass had fallen out and the cut that remained looked shallow. He found some roller gauze and dressed it.

Colby pulled a chair and sat next to her. This reminded him too much of how Brook had been toward the end of her life when treatment was no longer an option and she'd opted for hospice care. He'd spent many days just like this, beside her, a presence, to affirm to her that she was not alone.

Tentatively, he reached out and covered Regan's hand with his. It was cold. He glanced around the room and saw a blanket warmer, a small box resembling a microwave that held linens inside. He got up and pulled one out and tucked it around her body hoping for a greenhouse-like effect.

Sitting back down, he snaked his hand under the blanket and held her hand. "Regan," he said. No movement, but…did he see what he thought he saw?

Colby zeroed his eyes on the heart tracing. "Regan, it's Colby. Time to wake up." It was there—just the slightest upswing in her heart tracing. She'd heard him. Responded to him. Even if in the moment she couldn't open her eyes.

He lowered the side rail and rested his head on the mattress, kneading her hand with both of his. "Olivia needs you. Whatever is happening, you have to fight through it. Come back to me." He leaned forward and kissed the tips of her fingers. Could just his touch get her to open her eyes? He was willing to risk it—exposing his emotions physically if it brought her back to him.

Seeing Regan like this, so still and cold, brought forth all the emotions that he'd been trying to keep under wraps. That she was worth his putting his heart on the line again. He couldn't bear to just let her slip away like his wife. With cancer, sometimes there came a time when nothing could be done and it was best to let go.

But that wasn't now. Regan was strong.

The door opened and in walked Brian, holding Olivia's hand, Baldy a few steps behind him. At least the assault rifle was pointed down.

"I thought this was worth a try," Brian said.

He released Olivia's hand and backed out of the room. Baldy made of point of forcing Brian down the hall. Colby didn't know what to make of the scene—whether it was a ruse or not. His brain was tired of trying to calculate every contingency.

Colby wanted things to be simple and straightforward.

He pushed his chair back. Seeing her in the light versus the sealed black of darkness, Olivia Lockhart was a spitting image of her mother. Long auburn locks with streaks of darker red in her hair. Eyes, cornflower blue. Their eye color the only real difference between the two of them.

Colby reached his hand out to her. "Olivia, it's me. Colby. The same man who tried to help get away from these bad men a couple of nights ago. I'm still helping your mom." He waved her forward.

She responded, though unsurely. "What's wrong with her?"

"I'm not sure right now. I think she's just knocked out. Sometimes it takes a while to wake up."

Olivia kept walking until she stood directly next to Colby. "They keep telling me that she's going to leave me here alone."

"I think you're old enough to know the difference between good and bad people."

"Bad people kidnap you from your home."

"Exactly. When people do bad things then we can't trust what they say. We have to remember what the person has always done for us before."

Olivia nodded. "When will we get to go home?"

"I'm not sure." Colby patted his leg. "Want to try and talk to her?"

"She can hear me?"

Colby looked at the monitor and it was then he realized Regan's resting heart rate was up a good twenty points. Colby lifted Olivia onto his lap. "Yes, she can definitely hear you. You can hold her hand, too. Want to try?"

Olivia reached forward, much more bravely than Colby, and grabbed her mother's hand, placing her fingers in between Regan's and squeezing hard. "Mom!" A sweet singsong voice. "Let's go home. Can we go home?"

Olivia bent forward and kissed Regan's hand. "Time to get up, Sleeping Beauty." Olivia glanced back at Colby. "That's what she always says to me in the morning."

Colby smiled at Olivia's sweet innocence. No child should have to endure the things that Olivia had gone through. An abusive father. Grandparents that had disowned her. Colby reached out and put his hand on top of the two of theirs. Something in this moment felt inherently right. They all fit together.

"Thank you," Olivia said.

"For what?" Colby asked.

"For helping my mom—and for trying to help me."

"Do the bad men say anything to you?"

"They tell me that they aren't ever going to let me leave."

She'd confirmed what Colby had always suspected. It wasn't just about the cooler and what was in it. It was about Regan and what she knew.

"Do you think they tell the truth about anything?" Olivia asked.

"I don't know, why?"

"Because they told the truth about my mom, that she was sick, and that's why they're letting me visit with her. They also said that you'd be coming back here even if my mom got them what they wanted. They say I'll never see my home again."

A vacuous pit grew in Colby's stomach. It

didn't surprise him, these words spoken so innocently by Olivia but holding so much gravity for their future. The gunmen hadn't tried to hide their faces from them. Once they'd fulfilled their duty, they either had to keep them imprisoned or kill them. They were all expendable—eventually.

And if Regan didn't wake up soon, how long would they really keep any of them around? She had a lot to do in the next forty-eight hours.

The weight of danger became too much for Colby. "Regan, for all our sakes…open your eyes!"

His voice boomed, and Olivia shrank a little at the sound. He hadn't meant it to be that loud, but the desperation he felt carried in the volume of his voice, expressing the same amount of the distress he was feeling.

He felt it first. The slight squeeze to his hand. Olivia faced him again, her blue eyes bright with delight. "Did you feel that?"

"I did."

Colby risked glancing at Regan's face and was met with the gray-green eyes of a woman back from the edge.

Olivia climbed onto the bed and snuggled next to her mother.

Regan's eyes teared as she brought a hand

up and around Olivia's shoulders and squeezed her tightly.

She met Colby's gaze and mouthed, "Thank you."

The next second that the glass doors whooshed open and Ice Man grabbed Olivia and pulled her away from Regan.

"Now that you're awake, time to get back to work."

Everything in Regan's body hurt. Not a mild soreness, but more like she'd been spun in a cement mixer and then poured out under hot sun to harden. Vertigo made her feel like she was falling off the stool she was sitting on, and she gripped the metal corner of the table as a stabilizing force.

Emotions swirled almost as violently as her head. Olivia was alive—that was no longer a myth she clung onto for hope, and she whispered a prayer of thanks to God for answering her call. Knowing that should help her focus, but what Colby thought was an unwitnessed kiss—even if just to her fingertips—caused her to feel weak-kneed.

I have to concentrate. None of us will get out of here alive if I don't figure out something. Something that can fool these kidnappers into thinking that I'm giving them what they want.

The bad part was clear. What their hostage-takers asked for was impossible. Maybe *impossible* was not the right word—very improbable given the time frame.

Regan scooted the composition notebooks toward her on the table. The one that had taken the force of the explosion was tattered around the edges and smelled faintly of ash. Blood had seeped into the top of most of the pages, which stuck together as Regan tried to go through her notes. It was a little like going through an old photo album. These sequences she had first dreamed as potentially curing cancer had almost been naive, but she loved reliving the early yearnings of her career and the promise it held.

After scanning through each of the notebooks, Regan settled on the fact that some of the information could prove useful, but how could she use it enough to help her yet keep whatever they created nonlethal? Brian sat across from her at the table and had been eyeing her going through the pages without interjecting much.

She flipped to the middle of a different notebook, wondering if she could sequence something close to what they wanted. Something that would pass more rudimentary testing that could perhaps give them an opportunity to escape, but with a genetic kill switch in case she actually did create something unintentionally virulent.

Even that idea, though sound on the surface, she quickly discarded as hopeless. There just wasn't enough time.

"Can I show you something?" Brian asked.

Regan started. Had he been waiting for just the right opportunity to say something? "You have an idea?"

He motioned for the notebooks and she slid them across the table. After scanning the front labels, he picked one and turned quite directly to a particular genetic sequence.

"I think we need to start with this one," he said, pointing to the middle part of the page.

Regan pulled the notebook back her direction. Looking at the date entry of the notes, she timed it to four weeks before the lab accident. Why was Brian so interested in this entry? Why had he gone directly to it?

Regan closed the notebook and thrummed her fingers against the cover. What she absolutely had to do now was to keep her voice calm and steady when all she wanted to do was to stand, slap him across the face and yell words at him she'd never spoken since being a defiant teen. "Brian, did you change my protocol?"

Brian crossed his arms and leaned forward. "I was improving your concept."

Regan's vision coalesced. Everything she'd blamed herself for wasn't her fault at all. If Brian had changed anything about her protocol, he'd been the one to unleash the virulent strain. "But you can't remember how you changed it. You didn't write it down because you never wanted me to find out."

"You were always such a stickler for protocols—for making notes and cataloging experiments."

And now we know why. Because if you ignore protocols, bad things can and will happen, and people will die.

Her hope in keeping her voice measured was to prevent him from sensing her horror at what he'd done. "You know, I think the two of us together can do what they ask."

"You're...you're not mad?" he stammered, a look of relief clearing the haze that had been present in his eyes since they'd been in the cell together.

Now, for the risky part.

"I want in."

"Want in what?"

Regan leaned forward conspiratorially. "I know you're working with them."

She held her breath. The ultimate success or failure of her plan depended on his next words.

"How did you know?"

She smirked, hoping she was as good an actor as she was a doctor. "What tipped me off first was your needle prick site. If someone is struggling to get away from someone, it's not the easiest place to get injected. I can't believe you let them beat you up for effect."

Brian nodded—definitely proud.

Regan pushed on. "You know medicine isn't exactly what I thought it was going to be. Sure, I get some nice pats on the back for discovering this potential cure. Truth be told, human trials are still in the early phase, so who knows if it will pan out for sure. I'm a single mother and I'm *still* buried in debt from medical school. I want a different life for me and Olivia. I don't want to have to struggle financially through life. I want to give her everything she deserves."

Brian sat there for the longest time, staring at her. His elbows on the metal desk, his chin in his hands, he measured her with his green eyes like a human lie detector. "Honestly, this is hard for me to believe. You've always been above par. A Goody Two-shoes, as they say. Everything by the book. Now, all of a sudden, you're willing to break the law and become an international fugitive for some cash?"

A hole opened up in Regan's stomach. If she didn't sell this, the three of them would die. And there would be more deaths if she couldn't continue her research.

"Unfortunately, this incident and what I've already done is going to be the end of my career. I stole from a hospital—a cure they own intellectual property rights for. I'm the primary suspect in the murder of my nanny..."

The smug look that crossed Brian's face made Regan want to vomit what little she had in her stomach. Of course, she knew they had done it, but it seemed more than just removing an obstacle to their mission. Brian's look made it seem like he'd enjoyed it.

Problem was, if she acted like it affected her deeply, Brian was unlikely to buy the rest of her story. How could she speak when her throat had swelled to the point where it would squeak if she said one word?

So much senseless death all for financial gain. Was this what the world was now—or had it always been and now she was seeing its true nature fully revealed?

Brian continued to stare at her. Even though she wanted to get him to confess to Polina's murder, it wouldn't help her meet the goal she wanted. Regan had to get him to believe she'd crossed over from the Hippocratic oath that had ruled her life of doing no harm and wanted to become a hardened criminal.

"How much money?" Regan asked.

"You're looking for a cut?" Brian responded. "You can't accomplish what you want without me. We both know this will take more than a few days. I want accommodations—*nice accommodations*—for me and Olivia. I want a private tutor for her. I want security guards because there will be people looking for me. I want to live in a country without extradition agreements with the US. And I want at least twenty-five million dollars when I deliver the virus. Ten million up front."

Regan's heart pounded in her chest to the point she felt light-headed. Being this conniving was completely out of her character and it felt wrong to the very core of her being. Pain seared in her belly, but she returned his stare.

"You've been thinking a lot about this," Brian said.

Interesting. He hadn't said anything about the amount of money. Was the cash for this kind of venture limitless? Or was her demand low?

"I also want to stay with Olivia. No more locking me up. And I want freedom to access everything in the building."

Brian narrowed his eyes. Had she gone too far? Criminal negotiations were completely foreign to her. Colby would be much better at this. Not because he had a criminal mind but because as part of his career he was used to dealing with people who broke the law. He knew how they thought. How they communicated.

The thought perplexed her. Perhaps making the demands for free access had gone too far. Made him suspicious of her intentions.

"And what about your friend? What do we do with him?"

This part, she hadn't thought through. "Colby will help us." Would he? Surely he'd do whatever they needed to do to get out alive.

"The bounty hunter will help us."

Regan swallowed hard. "Absolutely."

Brian leaned back and folded his hands. How far up the hierarchy was he? Was he the ring leader of this whole operation? If so, Regan had completely underestimated his evil side. And if he discovered this whole thing was a ruse, there could be no end to the torture he would inflict upon them.

He splayed his hands on the metal surface. "I'll agree to most of your demands. You can see Olivia. We'll start to make arrangements for our US exit. You'll have to prove your words through action. There's no reason why you can't start your work on the virus. I'm not willing to go all the way yet and I'm not convinced Colby is the type who can be convinced to help us. But I might be persuaded at some point to add him to my protective detail—a man with his skills is hard to find. At night, you'll still be locked up. When I see that you're making progress as it relates to the virus, we'll give you more freedom. Until then, the three of you can be housed together. I'll work to get everything arranged."

"I can see Olivia now?"

"Not yet. Let me get everything transitioned."

"Then how about a tour?"

Brian nodded. It was in his eyes—he still didn't trust her, but he was willing to risk it to get what he wanted.

"Sure."

He stood and gestured for her to follow. He motioned to Baldy, who had been present in the lab, and he dropped his weapon.

Brian pushed through the two sets of lab doors. "Obviously you'll be restricted to the grounds. You won't be able to go past the fenced-in yard you've already visited."

He withdrew a ring of keys from his pocket. Cell keys? At some point she'd have to get those.

They stood outside the lab doors with three hallways. One in front, to the left and the right.

Brian motioned to her right. "Nothing down this hall that you need. Security personnel only. They'll get pretty twitchy if you head down there. Understood?"

Regan nodded.

"The door codes are all the same. Three fours and three twos. Most are push-button locks. Everything you need access to will have that type of lock. Everything else is off-limits."

Regan shifted on her feet.

"Straight ahead is the dormitory wing. It has a small suite of medical beds. They used to be used for large-animal autopsies. Outside that medical suite are the rooms where Olivia is. That's where we'll keep the three of you together—a close eye on the three of you. And to the left are the old animal cages where you've been staying."

"How long before I get to see her?"

Brian shrugged. "Not long if you're a good little doctor. If you do as you say, then we'll have you together by tonight."

"Thank you. I'm glad we could come to an agreement. Olivia and I can disappear. Lead a better life."

"Regan—you don't mind if I call you that, since we're partners now."

Regan's flesh prickled at the evil tinge in his voice.

"However, I do need to remind you that if you don't keep your word, I'll have no mercy when I end the lives of your daughter and your friend. You'll watch and then I'll slowly kill you. Understood?"

"Crystal clear."

FIFTEEN

Colby couldn't help but pace the cell. He was alone, and the longer he was isolated the more his mind raced down paths he didn't want to consider. As soon as Regan regained consciousness, they'd taken Olivia from her. The scene still caused his heart to grieve. Her reaching out. Olivia crying, asking to stay.

And then they'd hustled Colby out of the room and back into the animal cage where he felt like he was morphing into whatever primate they'd held here.

His thoughts were beginning to align with the large apes he saw when he visited the zoo. The violence and agitation. He wanted to hit something to dispel the electricity that zinged through his chest and tingled at the ends of his fingers.

Where was Regan? Was she okay? Were they hurting her?

The passage of time was hard to judge. His watch was long gone. There were no windows in the cell. No sunlight. He and Regan had definitely been separated for a few hours—but how many was hard to tell.

He peered out every angle of the cell to see if he could get any sense of what was happening. No one walked by. No guards. No sound. Nothing.

Have they taken them away and now I'm here alone?

He heard a door close. The snap of a lock. Soft footsteps and the click of steel-toed boots. He gripped the bars.

Please, Lord. Let this be Regan alive and unharmed. Bring her back to me.

The thoughts surprised him but also comforted him. His heart was ready, and he didn't want to lose her. Couldn't lose her. He had to keep her and Olivia safe—always.

When she came down the hall, she wasn't in zip-ties. Baldy didn't have a gun trained on her back. In fact, he was unarmed, as far as Colby could see. Something was different. There was a new measure of trust between her and the hostage-takers that maybe even extended to Colby.

What that signaled to Colby was that they were no longer worried about her taking off. Of course, holding Olivia's life over her head would likely ensure the compliance of any mother, but

Regan could easily break free and run if she wanted to try.

They seemed pretty confident that she wouldn't.

Baldy unlocked the cell, and she stepped in. He took a few steps back and then closed the door behind her.

Colby took her in, drank in every nuance of her physical appearance. Had they hurt her? No new bruising that he could see. She stood strong, tall, hair slightly disheveled. She remained in the same clothes they'd been given to go to the bank. She looked at him with questioning eyes, and he wanted to wipe the doubt away.

He took three steps and wrapped his arms around her, and she caved against his chest. He held her fast with one arm behind her back, the other cupping her head. He felt her body shudder under his hold.

Colby eased her back and wiped her tears with his thumbs. There were few words he could say to express exactly what he was feeling and his emotions took hold of his intellect. He leaned forward and brushed his lips against her cheek. Even with all they'd been through, her skin felt soft under his lips and he trailed them to her other cheek. He didn't want space or air between them, and he pressed her closer. She pushed back slightly and, at first, he feared she was pulling away, but then she looked up at him—her eyes clear, inviting, and he pressed his lips against hers.

Her lips were warm, soft. First tentative and then more confident.

Not where he'd imagined he'd first kiss her, but everything else was right about the moment. The physical expression of everything he'd been feeling over the past several days.

That he was at the point where he didn't want to live life without her and he was willing to let her know it.

Reluctantly, Regan pulled away and he smoothed his fingers over her lips—the pull between them still evident in his eyes. Colby smiled sweetly—almost as gently as the kisses he'd planted on her face and lips.

"I was worried," Colby said. "What happened?"

Regan took his hand in hers and eased them away from her face. She motioned them to the video camera in the corner of the room. "Do you think they can hear us in here?"

Regan doubted it, but this was also not her area of expertise. Nothing they talked about seemed to cause any repercussions. The hostage-takers didn't act privy to things Regan thought they had discussed confidentially.

"Probably video only. Enough to keep an eye

on us to make sure we're not trying to break out of here. Newly installed just for us by the looks of it."

"I didn't see any security cameras in the lab."

"I haven't seen any anywhere else, either. This is a decommissioned research facility. My guess is they were only worried about large animals escaping, which is the reason for the tower—an old, decrepit, wooden tower. Also, they probably wanted a watchful eye to keep people from coming onto the property."

"I made a deal," Regan said, breaking the flow of conversation.

"You did what?"

"Not a real deal—like a..."

"Ruse."

"Exactly. I told Brian I wanted in."

"And he bought it?" Colby asked.

Regan leaned against the wall, rubbing the back of his hand with her fingers, his hand so strong under her nimble one. Hands portrayed a lot about a person. Colby's signified strength and safety to her. She didn't want to lose the touch between them, either.

"I think so. Probably—at least enough to give me some access in the building. There's one wing they didn't want me to go down. Maybe that's where they're keeping weapons."

"Until we know for sure, it doesn't do me

much good to know if there might be some weapons in a room we don't know if I can get into."

"Brian has a set of keys. I'll figure out a way to get them from him. I think it holds some sort of master key to all these locks. Other doors have a punch code."

"How long are they planning on keeping us here?"

Regan shrugged. "The timeline isn't clear, but I insisted that we leave the country. I can't imagine they'd be able to put something together that quickly. Surely not before...the other thing happens."

The look on Colby's face wasn't something she expected—disappointment. He raked his fingers through his hair and paced around the cell. Had she done something wrong?

Finally, he stopped his restless wandering. "Tell me exactly what you told them."

"I asked for money. A lot of money. He didn't blink an eye."

"How much?"

"Twenty-five million. Ten million up front."

Colby let out a low whistle. Her skin prickled. "And they were fine with that amount?"

"Brian didn't argue with me."

"Which tells me you either low-balled them or they have no intention of paying it. The problem is if that amount of money is chump change then they could easily arrange for us to get out of here before our friends arrive. You know what they say about going to a secondary location."

"What?"

"Don't go," Colby stated.

"Why?"

"Because that's where you get killed."

"But aren't we already at the secondary location?"

Colby frowned. "If that was a joke, it's not funny. If we go outside the US, we'll be at the mercy of other foreign agents—whoever Brian's lined up to buy this virus. These are not nice people. They don't want or care to be reasoned with and they place no value on human life."

"Colby, it's not like I actually expected to leave. I had to get Brian to believe me, to gain his trust."

"Trouble is you might have set a timeline in place that will hinder our actual rescue."

SIXTEEN

Morning—day six. To say that Colby hadn't slept well through the night was an understatement. It had been more like periods of adrenaline-dried, comatose slumber interspersed with terror-filled nightmares. He didn't know how many times he'd woken up and reached across the distance between his and Regan's cots just to make sure she was still there. Now he watched her stir, her eyes slowly opening. She reached out her hand and held his.

Footsteps echoed down the hall. It was Brian with Baldy, who didn't have a weapon in his hands. Regardless of what Colby thought, Regan's ruse had seemed to instill some confidence that she'd be a compliant hostage.

Brian approached the bars. "Ready for your new quarters?"

Regan couldn't help but clap her hands together. "Olivia? Are you taking me to see her?"

"That's the plan." He turned his attention toward Colby. "Did Regan discuss our bargain with you?"

"I'm in complete agreement."

"Really? You'll become part of our security team? You'd be willing to kill for our mission?"

Colby didn't dare look at Regan's face. He could sense her pleading with him in her mind to not do anything to risk her not getting to see her daughter. If they were together, they would be better off when the compound was hit.

"I'd be willing to even provide some training to your team for the right amount of money. I'm former military—Special Operations Forces to be exact. I can make them even better than they are now."

Colby studied Brian's face the way a sniper studied a target through his scope, looking for any subtle notice that he was buying these fabrications. It wasn't in his nature to lie—he abhorred it—but right now it was necessary to get them out of this mess they were in.

One corner of Brian's mouth lifted slightly—a smirk. The reason behind the facial gesture could be good or bad. "You know, the two of you surprise me. Who knew you were such dark characters? I think I see us leading very posh lives as soon as we deliver what my buyers want."

Brian slid the key into the door and unlocked it. Baldy tensed for a moment but when Colby didn't immediately rush to get out, he seemed to relax.

"If you'll follow me, I'll take you to your daughter."

Regan stepped through the door. Colby moved to walk in front of her. As they made their way down the corridor, his head scanned side-to-side, constructing a mental map of the building in his mind.

Colby held his breath as he and Regan went through the door. Before he could even take in their surroundings, the door was locked behind them. Immediately, Olivia bounded up from her bed and ran into her mother's arms. Regan swept her up, planting kisses all over her face, setting her back down and pushing her to arm's length, giving a studied look of her daughter's appearance.

Then Regan placed one hand on each of her cheeks. "Olivia." She hugged her again. "Are you all right? Have they been taking good care of you?"

Olivia nodded her head and wrapped her arms around Regan's waist. "I missed you."

Colby turned away. One, to give Regan and her daughter a little privacy, but two, to fight the upswell of emotion within him because the picture of Regan and Olivia holding one another was what he could have had—wanted to have if

Brook hadn't been taken away from him. That moment between mother and daughter encompassed everything missing from his life. Everything he'd dreamed of having.

He felt a light tap on his shoulder and turned to see Olivia standing there. As soon as he turned, she wrapped her thin arms around him and squeezed with all her might. "I'm glad you're here."

A pain pierced Colby's chest. Not a feeling that signified hurt and loss but one that signified hope again for a future he could have. One that he'd once thought that he'd lost forever. He brought his arm protectively around her and hugged her gently. "I am, too."

Olivia pulled back. Colby glanced at Regan just as she wiped tears from her cheeks and offered him a gentle smile. Colby couldn't help but put himself in Regan's mind-set. How long had it been since both of them were treated the way they should by a man? How long had it been since they'd felt safe and protected?

Lord, help me help them. I've crossed over into this dangerous place where, if anything happens to them, I'll want to die, too. Give me the knowledge to figure out a plan to get us out of here safely. Let there be a life for us together.

He smiled to himself at the innocence and yearning of such a prayer. It was what he wanted.

He wanted Regan…and Olivia…he wanted all of them together.

"Mr. Colby—"

Colby laughed. The emotion lifted the tension from his chest. "Olivia, just call me Colby."

"Let me show you everything," she said.

Olivia took his hand and again he was overwhelmed by what he imagined to be a father's sense of duty to protect. He allowed her to lead him around the room, showing him the various things she had to entertain herself during her long periods of isolation. The high lilt of her voice drifted into the background as Colby assessed their quarters.

The room was fairly large. It looked like their captors had done some rearranging to keep them housed together. There were two cots placed perpendicular to Olivia's bed. Cheerful, pink, patterned pillows and blankets adorned the bed she'd been sleeping on. That was a conundrum for Colby. Why make Olivia more comfortable? Had the captors been planning on keeping them here indefinitely? Months? Years even? Had Regan's seeming willingness to want to be part of their plan changed their minds?

Olivia pulled him into the bathroom—a standing shower, toilet, sink and mirror. The mirror could be broken. Colby glanced behind him. A few towels. Those could be ripped to provide protection for his hand and he could make a rudimentary weapon from the linens and broken mirror pieces. There was also a towel rod. Colby reached up and yanked on it. It was slightly loose. A few good tugs and he could have it free to serve as another weapon.

Back in Olivia's room he noticed two windows set high near the ceiling. There was a small desk and chair where it appeared Olivia had entertained herself with some drawing and coloring. He grabbed the chair, placed in under the window and stepped up to see if it could form a way of escape.

There was no latch on the inside. The glass had wire mesh embedded in it, like you'd see in a prison. Plus, the windows were small. Not a viable option.

He scanned the ceiling. He couldn't see any cameras. Did these men truly trust that Regan and Colby would play along? The locked door to the room signified otherwise. It also didn't mean that there weren't listening devices. In fact, that was a real probability. They would be easier to hide in an enclosed room such as this versus the open space Colby and Regan had been held in before.

Colby noticed a radio on Olivia's desk. Interesting. He turned it on and scanned the channels. Finding a music station, he turned it up and motioned Regan toward him. She approached and he settled his hands on her waist, his heart stammering at their physical closeness. He brought one of his hands behind her neck and eased his lips next to her ear.

He whispered. "There could be bugs in here. When we talk about plans like this, the music is on. Whisper only."

Regan nodded.

"Your job is to find a way to get those keys. Look for weapons."

Regan pulled back and smiled.

Just as Colby turned the music off, there was a click at their door and Brian popped through.

"What do you think of your new accommodations?"

Colby tried to keep from fisting his hand. "They're definitely improved. Thank you."

"Great. Regan, you and I have some work to do. You'll be coming with me."

Olivia's eyes widened. "My mom's coming back here, right?"

"Of course, dear. Just as long as she and Colby do exactly what they've promised to do."

Regan walked on unsteady legs to the lab. She had violated the sales adage of underpromise and then overdeliver. She had definitely overpromised and now fresh fear revved up her anxiety to somehow pull off her, Colby, and Olivia's great escape—or at least a way to stay alive until the military arrived, which should be noon tomorrow.

There was much to be apprehensive about. She still faced prosecution if she didn't provide a list of names to Nicholas as far as buyers went.

Once inside the lab, Brian pulled a notebook where he'd been manipulating some of the early versions of her modified polio virus to see if he could get it to do the deadly things he aspired to do—or least earn him the money he wanted.

Regan used her finger to scan over the formulations. Good news, they certainly weren't dangerous. The manipulations were some she'd tried and had previously failed. "I think you're off to a good start. Maybe we should have a different focus."

"What do you mean?"

Regan motioned to their surroundings. "This isn't an ideal place for these experiments. How long before we're discovered here? You're only a few hours outside Denver."

"It's an old top-secret research lab constructed by the military during WWII and decommissioned only after the international treaty was signed in the 1970s. You don't think they performed biological weapon experiments here?"

Brian's tone was edgy, almost as if she'd slapped him across the face.

Regan couldn't help herself. "Brian, regardless of what they used to do here, this isn't a level 4 containment unit. When we create the airborne polio, we'll be the first to die. We're not wearing anything that will protect us."

Brian pounded his fist into the desk and several glass flasks toppled over. Regan started. He turned away from her and paced away, punching one fist into his other palm.

Great. Just what I need. A testy, volatile man who doesn't understand the basics of microbiology. Now I'm sure the accident at my lab was his fault.

Having no sense of ethical boundaries or safe lab procedure was a deadly mix for everyone. Above all else, she had to keep him from conducting experiments on his own. *How do I get him to settle down?*

"Brian, I'm sorry. Come sit down. Let's talk this through."

He turned back to her and huffed all the way to the lab stool like a petulant toddler she'd just released from time-out.

"Do you know where we're going yet? What country?" Regan asked.

"I've made arrangements. I know they'll have…what we need."

"Meaning containment."

"Yes. Let's just say they're known for their work using virulent agents."

Regan smiled, hoping it seemed warm and genuine and didn't portray the horror that percolated in her gut. "Excellent. You didn't mention what country that is."

Brian smirked. "I'm still not sure about you, Regan. Whether or not I can trust you. Maybe it's better if you didn't know."

"I'm surprised that you would say that. You know as well as I do that my regular life is over. This is the only path for Olivia and me to have a good life. If I go back, make any sort of public appearance again, I'll be arrested. I doubt I'd have much chance of acquittal based on the likely charges against me and, even if they don't put me in jail for the rest of my life, I'll never be a doctor again."

Regan reached out, covered Brian's hands with her hers and tried to summon every desperate thought in her mind—which wasn't hard considering her circumstances. These words had to convince Brian that her fate was aligned with his when she'd truly aligned herself with Colby.

"You're my only hope, Brian. Please, trust me to do the things I said I would."

Brian eased his hands out from under hers and reached into the pocket of his lab coat. He pulled out a small red notebook. "We're going to the Middle East." He opened his notebook. There was a list of names with money amounts next to each one.

Regan pressed her lips together. No wonder Brian hadn't balked at her amount. It was about five percent of the amounts she was seeing on the page. Obscene amounts of money. Was there no limit in man to pay for evil?

Brian tapped the page with his finger. "This is the list of all the interested buyers, but the amount they'll pay is contingent upon when we deliver the product. I've been working with a man who has ties to all these entities and is working to get the best price."

The broker. So Nicholas was right.

Brian continued. "He says he'll protect us and allow us to work at his compound. I can't say I entirely trust him, but I think he's the best choice at this moment. The sooner we deliver the bioweapon, the more money he'll be able to get, but I'm not the only scientist he's making deals with. Perhaps just the one with the most promising biological agent."

"What do you mean?" Regan asked.

"Just what I said—there're other interested contractors. Whoever delivers first gets the most money." Ryan flipped to another page in his book. "These are the other people I know who are trying to create a bioweapon for sale."

Regan glanced at the list. That book was her Get Out of Jail Free card. It had everything Nicholas Abrams wanted—more than he wanted. Not only would he be able to identify the interested parties, but they could also work to shut down production.

Brian closed the notebook and tucked it back in his pocket. It jingled next to the set of keys Regan desperately wanted to acquire. "Let's just say I don't trust computers to keep the information safe. Computers can be hacked."

But notebooks can be stolen.

He stood from the table. "I think you're right, Regan. Preparation is the key. We do need to start gathering up the items we need from this facility." Suddenly he reached for his pants pocket and pulled out a phone. After scanning the message, he began to walk away from her. "I'm needed elsewhere. You'll find some boxes in one of the back closets." He stopped and stared at her. "This is your first test, Regan. Don't disappoint me. I better find you here when I return." The door closed behind him.

Regan stood there for a few minutes. Would he immediately come back? Several doors slammed and she heard the noise of car engines starting, which drew her to the window.

Brian, Baldy and Ice Man had piled into an SUV and were driving off the property.

Was she alone? Really alone?

SEVENTEEN

The sound of the SUV's engine roaring to life pulled Colby's attention to the window. He grabbed the chair from the desk, climbed up and peered through the dusty glass. He counted the occupants. Three. Could it be all of the hostage-takers? Had they really left the inmates in charge of the asylum? He peered to his right at the guard tower. Still one man present, serving as a lookout. His body type didn't remind him of anyone they'd met yet. The man paced back and forth with a long rifle across his chest.

"What are you doing, Colby?" Olivia asked.

"I think the bad guys just left."

Before he could step down, there was a rattle at knob. A shiver ran through Colby and he took hold of Olivia's arm, as gently as he could to not frighten her, and pulled her behind him. Who could this be? An assassin left to do them in? What part of the plan had changed?

The door burst open and Colby exhaled, dropping his hands to his knees.

Regan. Olivia ran out from behind Colby's legs to hug her.

"I don't know how much time we have, but let's start looking around this place," Regan said.

"You didn't see anyone between the lab and this room?" Colby asked.

Regan shook her head. "No. We should leave… right now."

Colby shook his head. "That's not going to work. There's still one guard in the tower with likely a three-hundred-and-sixty-degree view of the complex. All we'd be is target practice."

"Then we need to figure out what we can use inside this building. Figure out some contingency plans."

Colby couldn't help but smile. *My thoughts exactly.*

Regan turned for the door, but before Colby could take a step forward Olivia reached back and took his hand. It halted his steps at how natural it felt—the trust she was placing in him to protect her.

Regan caught the gesture and her eyes spoke volumes, as if it pleasantly surprised her that Olivia could trust an adult male so easily after what she'd been through. It didn't surprise Colby.

Kids were smart. They were instinctual creatures. Often times, they could get the real lay of the land before most adults.

"I think we should check out that hallway where I thought the firearms might be kept. Let's see what kind of arsenal we have access to," Colby said.

"Good idea."

"By the way, how did you get in here?"

Regan raised her hand. "I found a master key in the lab."

Colby frowned. Interesting. Either Regan had really earned their trust with her ruse or they had become careless for some reason. Colby was beginning to think it was the latter because of their hasty departure.

Reluctantly, Colby let go of Olivia's hand. "Let me go first." He stepped in front of the duo. "Stay behind me. I'll motion you forward if the coast is clear."

"But you don't know the way," Regan pointed out.

"It not hard. We're in a basic cross shape. The lab is directly ahead. The forbidden hallway is to our left, correct? Our old cell was to the right."

Regan smirked. "Right. Or correct. Or whatever the proper former-military-bounty-hunter lingo might be."

"Affirmative," Olivia said. "That's the word you'd use?"

"Affirmative," Colby said, and eased the door open.

The first hallway was clear. Colby moved with light feet but the clicking sound from Regan's high heels was like Morse code tapping away an announcement to their location. Colby turned back, pointed to her feet and sliced his index finger across his neck. Regan responded with a quizzical look.

He mouthed, "Shoes. Off."

Regan slid the footwear from her feet and tucked them to the side. There wasn't really any place she could hide them. Olivia wore tennis shoes, and her footsteps were silent.

Colby proceeded forward. They came to the cross section. The hallway he was interested in investigating was closed off by a set of heavy metal doors, but they had mesh windows he could look through. Colby motioned for Regan and Olivia to stay put.

After checking in both directions—he didn't see anyone—he bounded forward to the door and glanced through the window, his heart hammering in chest. This whole outing was risky. If they were caught, not only could their only decently crafted cover story be blown, but the betrayal their captors would feel could be enough to incite them to murder.

Colby exhaled slowly. No one was present. He nudged the door gently—it gave way and no alarm sounded.

He pushed the door open wider and waved Olivia and Regan forward. Both sprinted in his direction. Once they'd come across the threshold, Colby eased the heavy metal door closed. A faint whoosh sounded as it seated into the door frame.

From the hall, there were no windows outside. Before them were four doors. Three had round doorknobs. One had a punch code.

Colby pushed away from the wall and tested the first door. It opened easily. Regan and Olivia followed him inside.

A staff lounge. At least, that was what it reminded Colby of. Two round, white, Formica-topped tables. Five plastic chairs at each. A row of lockers. Some with combination locks. A large television was mounted on one wall, and the first thing Colby wanted to do was to turn it on to see if he could find any local news that discussed Regan. Had the media at this point tied the two of them together?

There was a large picture window. He peered outside. From his vantage point, he couldn't see the guard tower. Hopefully the man was still watching the perimeter and had little interest in what was happening inside.

There was a closet with a bifold door. Regan stepped up and pulled it open.

"They look like employee mailboxes," she said. She riffled through some papers and then closed the door. "Nothing too interesting. Paycheck stubs." She picked one up and scrutinized it. "They look to be issued by a legitimate bank."

"We should write down all the information on that check," Colby said.

"Don't you think it would be odd that they'd be paid by something so easily traceable?" Regan asked.

"Maybe they've maneuvered themselves through a legit company. Hard to know at this point. All we're really gathering is a few pieces to the puzzle. Abrams probably has a lot of the big picture, but he's not going to let us in on it. Not yet, at least. Maybe never."

Regan nodded and began scanning for pen and paper. Colby began to go through the open lockers. Mostly warm-weather clothing. Either remnants from staying there for a few months or they were prepping for a long stay.

He tried some simple combinations on the locks. One he successfully opened just using one-two-three-four. A jacket. At the bottom, a leather wallet. One handgun without bullets.

A coil of detonation cord. All useful items but without the necessary components to make them functional. He pulled the wallet out and opened it. A driver's license was present.

Regan had found a small tablet and pen.

"Might as well add this information to your notes." Colby flipped the license onto the table.

Once she was done copying the information and had placed the items back, Colby motioned them into the hall. The door to the room directly across from the staff lounge was unlocked, as well. Colby peered into the darkened room and palmed the wall by the door frame for a light. He turned it on.

What he saw looked like some medieval torture chamber.

Regan stood on her tiptoes and peered over his shoulder. "Medical equipment."

Colby stepped aside. "Anything we can use in here?"

"Looks like they did quite a bit here at one point—medically speaking." Regan slapped the top of a metal box with numerous numbers and dials. "This is a ventilator. An old one. Probably one of the first ones ever made, which seems consistent with the time frame of this facility—the 1970s." She motioned beside her. "These are defibrillators. Seems to be that whatever they were doing they didn't necessarily want the experiments to end in death."

"That's not exactly comforting. What, they infect something and...?"

"See if the cure works and, if it doesn't, can they resuscitate and try something else. Sometimes treatments have a synergistic effect. Give one thing in isolation, it doesn't help. But add two things together and they help the other one work even better."

"Like you and me." The sentence slipped from Colby's lips before his mind engaged as to what the consequences of those four words might be. He froze.

Olivia stepped up next to him and laid her head against his side. "What about me?"

"A cord of three strands..." Regan said softly.

"Is not easily broken," Colby replied.

The verse he'd once learned came to the forefront of his mind. How long had it been since he'd heard it? Years. Maybe a decade or longer. Of course, there was the biblical meaning of two with God, but as Colby looked at the three of them, it was beginning to feel more and more like God had put them in this instance together. For a reason. His skill set. Regan's knowledge. Olivia's upbeat spirit despite what she'd been through. Together they had the skills to survive this.

Regan turned away and began rummaging through the equipment. She opened one large metal cabinet and pulled out a tranquilizer gun. "There are four of these in here as well as what appear to be darts. Would you know how to use them?" she asked.

"Anything that shoots something out of it has basic functions that translate from weapon to weapon."

"That's not what I asked."

Colby smiled teasingly. "What I meant to say in a somewhat intelligent way was that I can figure it out. Did you find any medication to go with it?"

"Not that I see for now. Maybe in the lab. We still need to go through everything in there."

"Anything else in the cabinet?" Colby asked.

"Bags of IV fluid." Regan picked one up. "Not even expired."

Colby's skin prickled. At first, finding old medical equipment wasn't surprising, but to find medications that weren't expired meant to him that they were planning for a lot of contingencies. On possibly keeping injured people alive.

But there were other things those IV bags of solution could be used for.

"We can make bombs," Colby stated.

Regan eased the door closed—her face slightly pale. Colby understood her plight. Living through violence was one thing. Causing it, especially as a physician, was another thing.

"Out of IV fluids?" Regan asked.

"Those bags combined with the det cord I found in that guy's locker would build a rudimentary bomb. We'd just need to find something to light it."

Regan peered back into the space. "There's nothing like that here. All that remains is resuscitation equipment. Syringes. Needles. A fully stocked medical supply cabinet minus the medications."

"Either they've been here awhile or planned to stay awhile. Hard to know for certain. Let's figure out if there's anything of value in the other rooms."

Colby leaned back and checked down the hall. No one visible. He motioned them out. The next room was empty. The fourth one was locked with a punch code.

Regan stepped up and tried a few combinations without luck. "Time for the lab," she said.

Regan pushed through the lab doors.

First thing to search through was the bank of freezers. There were vials and petri dishes. Some had unidentified specimens growing in them—nothing likely airborne, or at least nothing with a short incubation period, or she'd already be sick.

Olivia and Colby hovered near. "The two of you should step back just in case I spill something that could cause an infection."

Or flat-out kill us.

Colby took Olivia's hand and walked to the widows near the back of the lab.

Regan's heart fluttered wildly. He was so natural with her, and Olivia seemed to trust him implicitly. Her normally pensive wall around men crumbled in Colby's presence. Was the guard still in the tower? Colby didn't give any indication that he was worried.

Turning her attention back to the freezers, she continued to scan their contents. Most were empty. One cabinet held drugs—a few vials of a paralyzing agent were present. Regan pocketed one, hoping that leaving the rest would seem like she hadn't pilfered one from the stock. It could be beneficial if loaded into a dart if they used one of the animal tranquilizer guns. The problem was it would be death for whoever was injected with it unless lifesaving medical treatment was provided. The drug ceased all muscle function—including the muscles used for breathing, but the person remained awake. The victim suffocated to death with full awareness of what was happening.

It went against everything she believed in as a physician, and a dark pit of fear began to seed itself in her chest. There was no denying that at some point she might have to actively participate in hurting someone else to save Olivia.

To save Colby.

Could she do it?

Pushing the thought from her mind, she hit more cabinets that sat above the sinks next to the freezers. There were more medications. Morphine. Ketamine. These could knock a person down and, if administered in the right dose, shouldn't stop their breathing. In a drawer, Regan found several syringes. The ketamine was probably the best choice: it could be given in the muscle. But the problem was that it took time to act. As long as ten minutes before a person was incapacitated, but at least the person's life would be spared.

The question was, could she keep herself alive until the drug kicked in? Regan put a syringe and the drug vials in her pocket and pulled out her tucked-in shirt to cover it.

The next room was Brian's office. Colby had taken a chair and found a piece of paper and a pen and was engaged in some sort of game with Olivia. From inside Brian's office, Regan couldn't help but smile. He was so natural with her. Unlike her ex-husband who'd always seemed so uncomfortable around Olivia—even before the abuse started.

I want this picture as part of my life. The three of us together. Can it ever happen? Will we be able to get through this?

Regan leafed through the papers on Brian's desk. When she opened one manila folder her heart stalled and she felt light-headed. She pulled the chair out from the desk and sat, her fingers trembling as she scanned through the pages.

It was easy to view Brian as weak because physically he was slim and of average height. He seemed easy to take advantage of because of his quiet nature. She'd never witnessed a hint of deviousness in him the whole time they'd worked together—only her suspicions.

Perhaps it was true what they said about the quiet ones—that they were always hiding something.

Sometimes good things.

Sometimes evil, nefarious things.

Regan held photos of Polina in her hands. One was marked with a heavy black X crossed through her face. Regan pressed her arm against her stomach. He had to pay for this. Had to pay for all of it. For Polina's death. For risking Olivia's life. For risking the lives of her patients and the treatment that could save them. Anger smoldered.

Another folder held news clippings and internet articles about Regan's career. Wherever her name had been printed, someone had inserted text next to Regan's name. Handwritten, like an editor's correction, that said "and Brian Hollis." The notations resembled Brian's handwriting. Almost as if he wanted his name forever paired with hers. Definitely professionally, but could he have had some romantic interest in her, as well? Is that why he was so willing to let her in on this deal?

Other folders held documents written in languages she couldn't understand. Some of the type looked Russian. Others Arabic. Evidence that Brian was speaking the truth about his intentions. He really was lining up buyers for whatever weapon they could create.

Suddenly she saw Colby stand and back away from the window. He waved frantically to her. "The guard is climbing down off the tower. We need to get back to where we were."

Colby and Olivia ran through the lab doors. Regan followed, pulling the key from the opposite pocket that held the syringe and needles. They ran down the cement hall back to the room that had held Colby and Olivia.

Olivia ran through first. Colby turned and cupped Regan's face with his hand. "Stay safe."

What she wanted was to feel his closeness again, but she backed away, pushed the door closed and heard the click of a heavy lock engaging. She was steps from the lab door when she realized that her shoes were still in the hall outside their prison cell.

Turning on her heel, Regan sprinted as quickly as she could on quiet toes and grabbed the shoes. She could hear boot steps on the concrete. When she came to the cross of the two main halls, the lab doors immediately in front of her, she peered down the hall, her hearing muffled by the sound of blood rushing, and she saw one man walking away from her toward the animal enclosures.

She sprinted across the hall and into the lab and settled herself on one of the stools. From a distance came a steady thump-thump of helicopter blades. According to her and Colby's calculations, the military wasn't arriving until tomorrow midday.

Could they be coming now? Could this whole ordeal be over? Regan went to the window where Colby had previously held his vigil and fingered open two slats of the cheap metal blind. A military-type helicopter landed. Brian, Baldy and Ice Man stepped out while the blades still whirled. They hustled their way into the building. Doors opened. Banged closed.

Regan was walking back to the desk that held her notebooks when she remembered the piece of paper Colby and Olivia had been drawing on.

Quickly, she ran back and scooped the sheet

up, folded it, and quickly tucked it into the back pocket of her slacks.

She ran back to the lab table and sat, whisked open one of the notebooks and tried to act as if she'd been pouring over them the whole time Brian had been gone.

He burst through the doors so hard they clanged against the walls.

"We need to pack up. We're leaving."

"Why?"

"Some of my informants are concerned that this site has been leaked to the military and that an assault on the compound is coming in the next couple of days."

Regan swallowed hard. How was it possible? Who could have leaked the information? One of Abrams's men? Did Nicholas have a mole he didn't know about? Or was it the trackers they had swallowed? Had that alerted their captors?

"When?" Regan asked, hoping her voice didn't betray how anxious she was.

"Two hours."

"What about Olivia? Colby?"

"What's most important right now is you and what's in this lab. Help me start packing."

Regan's throat tightened. Whatever Brian's plan was, it didn't include the two most important people in her life.

They were going to die if Regan didn't do something to stop him.

EIGHTEEN

Regan stood stock-still as Brian began pacing around the lab. He stopped at a closet, pulled open the door and yanked out several folded-up cardboard boxes.

"You need to help me. What do you think is the most important thing we should take?"

Adrenaline poured into Regan's blood. *I can't believe I'm even considering doing this. Can I do this? Can I incapacitate Brian?*

"The notebooks, of course," Regan said.

From the closet, Brian pulled a couple of rolls of packing tape and threw them onto the closest lab table. "Of course." He turned and smiled at her. "I can't believe this is really happening!" His voice didn't give off a hint of betrayal, but rather excitement.

"We'll finally be together. We'll be rich! Richer than either of us thought possible slaving away in that lab for years."

Perhaps her thinking was correct about Brian

had envisioned a personal relationship budding between the two of them if he could keep her confined and forced to interact with him.

An emotional prison could be just as confining as a physical one. Olivia's father had used words and his hands. Regan could have freely left, but the trauma from his onslaught had kept her chained for a long time just as easily as a pair of handcuffs. She'd been in prison before. She wasn't going back. And certainly not with Brian. Whatever his plan was, she couldn't allow them to leave the facility.

It would be the place of her last stand in this nightmare.

Regan stood straighter and the plan in her mind firmed up. "I'll go see what cultures we need from the freezers. You have a way to transport them?"

"Ah, yes. I have plenty of coolers and dry ice. Did you see that I had some variations that I wanted you to check while I was gone? Not airborne, but I think they're definitely more virulent than regular polio. Isn't that the weirdest term? *Regular polio.*" Brian chuckled to himself.

Regan's blood ran cold.

She walked back to the space that held the freezers. She opened one of the units, the one that held all the existing petri dishes, pulling the syringe from her pocket before she knelt down.

With her back turned to Brian, she rustled the syringe out of its package and threw the wrapper into the bottom of the freezer. She then pulled the three vials from her pocket. The spilling mist helped hide her movements. Despite her fear, she couldn't use the paralyzing agent. She couldn't kill Brian. That left morphine or ketamine. She grabbed the ketamine and discarded the other two drugs.

Pulling the cap off with shaky fingers, she plunged the needle into the clear liquid and drew up three milliliters of the ketamine. That dose should definitely be enough to incapacitate him. The problem would be keeping Brian from killing her until the drug took hold.

Regan stood and pushed the bared needle through the bottom of the pocket of her lab coat. The metal could easily be seen if Brian was looking for it. She bent over, grabbed a stack of petri dishes from the freezer and walked back to Brian, setting them on the lab table and unstacking them so they sat side by side.

"I think these are the best ones to take. How about you?"

He fastened one more piece of packing tape to the bottom of a box and flipped it over. From his pocket, he pulled out a pair of reading glasses and began to examine the notations on the cultures.

As he leaned over, Regan pulled the syringe out of her pocket.

"Is this some kind of joke?" Brian asked.

Regan tucked the syringe behind her back just as he straightened.

Her eyes widened—a natural response when someone attempted to look as innocent as a kid with her hand in the cookie jar. "What do you mean?"

He motioned his hand across the plastic containers. "These aren't even polio."

Regan's stomach knotted. Her next action was going to feel as unnatural as anything she'd ever had to do in her life. She stepped closer to Brian. "Why just stick with polio?"

"What do you mean?"

"I'm sure you've heard about what other foreign governments are doing. Cross-breeding certain highly virulent agents into their own creations."

He eased back from her, one corner of his lip slightly downturned. "You'd want to do something like that?"

Regan placed her hand on his shoulder and pulled him gently toward her. "Do you think it would bring more money?"

Brian's smirk turned into a smile. He eased his hand behind her back and rested it between her shoulder blades, pulling her gently toward his body, nestling his face against her neck. "Did you have something specific in mind?"

Acid wormed its way up Regan's throat. "Just this."

Regan brought her hand up and thrust the needle into Brian's shoulder with one hand, using her other arm to grab him around his back to hold him close to her as long as she could.

Sometimes keeping the enemy within reach was the easiest way to control them.

She pressed the top of the syringe so hard that the tip of her thumb numbed under the pressure and she managed to get most of the dose in before Brian's mind tuned in to her betrayal and he shoved her into the metal lab table. She whiplashed backward—the table at her waist, her head making contact. Her vision fuzzed and she heard the dishes scatter to the floor, knowing their tops popped off, spilling their contents into the open air.

Before Regan could right herself, his hands were around her neck. The cold metal of the lab table bit into her back and her feet scrambled to find purchase on the floor. She clawed at his fingers wrapped tightly around her neck. The pain of her fingernails gouging into his skin seemingly fueled his strength and, impossibly, he squeezed his hands tighter. She pulled her knees up and kicked out into his belly to knock him backward. The force did little to knock him off his feet, but did loosen his grip enough that she was able to take several lungfuls of air as she flipped her body to the side and pulled herself off the table.

As she crashed onto the concrete floor, Brian's grip broke. Regan scrambled forward, pulling lab stools down in her wake to make further obstacles. She briefly turned around and found him on his knees trying to clamber over the stools with awkward, stilted movements, like a baby just learning to crawl.

In one last attempt he heaved his body forward and clasped onto her ankle with a grip that still had a fair amount of strength. Regan flipped onto her back and pulled her foot toward her with all her strength. A couple of good yanks and she was free.

Her vision blurred and she laid her head against the concrete.

That was when she heard the pounding of boots on the cement, coming straight for her.

The whir of the helicopter blades cutting through the air pulled Colby's attention to the window. He barely caught a glimpse of the aircraft as it passed by. In the flash he saw a faint glimpse of something that could be military but, in all honesty, he was speculating.

Whatever it was, he was worried. He looked over at Olivia. Ice Man keyed through the door, and Colby stepped down off the chair. Without requesting her to, Olivia scurried to Colby's side and he placed a protective arm around her shoulder.

There was a hint of something in the man's eyes that didn't bode well for Colby and Olivia. He'd seen it before in many men—a combination of madness and determination. His jaw was set, the muscles taut at the sides of his face, and his eyes were matted dark, like the last ember of goodness had been consumed by the blackness of the deed he'd come to do.

Even Olivia, a young girl with years' less experience, sensed the same thing Colby did, and her body shook next to his. He squeezed her shoulder reassuringly even though calm was the last thing he felt.

Ice Man and Colby stared at one another as if facing off in an old-fashioned duel—except Colby was unarmed. Colby glanced around the room quickly. Was there anything he could use as a weapon that could be effective against an automatic weapon?

Ice Man's right shoulder twitched and Colby propelled Olivia to the ground, took two steps and jumped into the air, hitting the man square in the chest before he could raise his weapon.

Colby grappled him in a bear hug, the weapon trapped between them. Ice Man wiggled his arm free and was able to place his hand on the trigger.

"Olivia! Get under the bed!"

From Colby's vantage point, he couldn't see Olivia clearly, but he heard rustling and hoped it was her dive-bombing for cover.

Ice Man pressed the trigger and bullets released from the tip of the weapon in a hail fire of fury, spraying into the wall and knocking down plaster.

Colby's heart thudded wildly in his chest. His ears rang. Was Olivia screaming? He couldn't distinguish between that and the high pitch of injured eardrums. If he didn't fix this situation quickly, they were both going to die.

Colby eased up slightly and placed both his hands on the gun and then flipped over. The man arced over him and, as Ice Man was airborne, Colby pulled the weapon free from his hands. He then scrambled to his feet, turning the gun around before his attacker could right himself, and pummeled the end of the gun into the man's head. His body fell limp and Colby hit him again for good measure.

Colby used the strap to shoulder the weapon and began to disassemble Olivia's bed so he could get to the sheet. Using his teeth, he quickly tore several strips of cloth. He flipped the man over onto his stomach, grabbed his hands and wrapped the butterfly-print strips several times around his wrists, tying the binds tightly.

Colby then bound Ice Man's feet. "Olivia. It's okay. You can come out."

Her hand ventured out from beneath the bed. It was as bright and pale as a full moon on an autumn night. She whimpered.

Colby finished binding the man's ankles and began to rifle through his pockets. He found what he'd hoped for. A lighter. Their prison key.

Nothing else other than the weapon proved useful.

Once Olivia had her head out from under the bed and saw the man was incapacitated, she scrambled into Colby's arms. He held her tightly and everything that had been emotionally closed off since his wife's death sprang open like a dam at flood stage.

Tears coursed down his cheeks and he hugged her tightly with one arm and smoothed his other hand over her tousled hair. With everything in him, he wanted to speak soothing words. To tell her it was going to be all right, but he was never one able to lie.

My own lost daughter would have been Olivia's age right now.

One loss he had never fully grieved was his daughter not ever being born. All that he had missed. Her first smile. Her first words. Would it have been *mama* or *dada*? Crawling. Walking. Taking her to kindergarten. Giving her away to the man of her dreams.

Colby bit his lip, hoping the pain would stop this flow of tears. He had to pull himself together. None of them was safe yet. He had to find Regan. Was she still alive?

He swallowed hard. “Olivia, we’re okay.” He pushed her back and thumbed the tears away from her cheeks, the pink slowly returning.

She placed her hands over his and squinted her eyes closed. “Thank you.” She popped them open, the pale blue vibrant. “Colby, please, don’t leave me.”

“I won’t.”

I can’t.

Were those words just for now or were they for forever?

NINETEEN

Colby pulled Olivia behind him, scanning the cross hallway and finding no one coming down the path. He placed two bullets in the coded lock and burst through the lab's door.

Adrenaline began to leak through his body like water through sand and he felt the strength leave his muscles. At first, he didn't see anyone.

Then he saw the tousled components on top of the counter, the overturned chairs. He ran that direction and saw two bodies lying on the ground. Brian, something clearly wrong with him, was making ineffectual body movements, like a slug trying to slither through molasses. His eyes ticked back and forth like a metronome.

Colby grabbed Brian by the ankles and pulled him back. Regan was moving, her fingers at her forehead. Colby kneeled next to her and grabbed her hand.

"Regan, it's Colby—"

Her eyes popped open. "Olivia?"

"She's here." He looked at Olivia. "Your mom's okay." He turned back to Regan. "What happened?"

"Brian said he knew the military was coming. He was getting ready to escape with just me and some of the stuff from the lab."

"Is he dead?" Colby asked.

Regan eased to a sitting position and swayed slightly. "No. Ketamine. He can't move—but it's not going to last long. Thirty minutes at a minimum."

Colby heard the roar of two car engines and scuttled to the window. Through the blinds he could see two Jeeps of armed men. Four new foes altogether. He scrambled back to Regan. "Up you go. We need to see what kind of weapons we can get our hands on."

Regan got to her feet and pressed two fingers into her temple. "Dizzy."

Colby grabbed her hand and eased her forward as much as she could tolerate. "Concussion, probably, but I guess I don't need to tell you that."

He scurried them into the locker room. "I need to get the det cord out of that locker." He tried to recall which one it was. First one he opened was a no go. In the second he found the treasure he was looking for. He grabbed it. "I need you to get a bag of the IV fluid."

At the door, he scanned the hall. A couple of

men marched his way. He pulled back into the locker room and pressed his ear against the door. They were fading away—likely going to the cell that had held him and Olivia. That meant they would find their injured comrade and discover Colby was alive.

They were losing time to escape, and fast.

Colby peeked out the door again and saw the hall was vacant. He hustled them across the space and into the medical supply room. Regan clambered toward the metal cabinet and pulled out a bag. Colby grabbed it from her and motioned them back into the hall.

Regan huddled next to Olivia at the edge of the hall as Colby constructed a rudimentary bomb out of their pilfered items. From his pocket, he lit the fuse and motioned them back into the medical equipment room.

He huddled them together. "Once that goes off, everyone is going to come running our way. Just do as I say when I say it. Don't overthink it. I'm hoping there's some good stuff in that room to help us. If not, all we have is this gun."

Regan nodded and gripped Olivia's hand. *Lord, we need Your help. All of us. If there's any way You can see to get us out of this alive and in one piece, then—*

The explosion was louder than Regan imagined it would be, and the vibration rattled her bones. Colby opened the door, took a quick glance, and the three of them poured through the door to the room that as of yet had been unexplored. The door hung on its hinges, swaying brokenly in the wake of the concussive blow. They piled into the room. Colby opened several of the cabinets. He grabbed a handgun. He found a bag and loaded it with several rounds of ammunition.

When Colby opened the next cabinet he pumped his fist into the air like a boy who'd got exactly what he wanted for Christmas. What he pulled out looked to be a rocket launcher.

"Yes! Hold this." He laid it in her arms, and she bent slightly under the weight. Colby continued to search through the cabinets until he stood with two large pieces of ammunition held in each hand. "We just might survive this."

First, Colby threw the small bag of ammunition over his neck and snuck his arm through so it was easily accessible for his right hand. He then secured the automatic weapon over one shoulder so it sat crosswise in front of his chest. The handgun was placed in the band of his jeans at the small of his back.

Colby took the weapon from her and motioned to the corner of the room. "We're going out that door."

Regan smiled weakly. A boy and his toys—the same amount of jubilation regardless of the level of danger.

Just as Colby shouldered through the door, a screeching alarm sent needles of fear through Regan's body.

If the explosion hadn't disclosed their location, then the alarm certainly would.

Colby huddled against the building. The assault rifle across his chest left his hand available for the rocket launcher.

"What's your plan?" Regan asked.

"I'm hoping they'll stay busy inside the compound looking for us and we can make it to one of those Jeeps and drive off the property."

He shifted the assault rifle so it felt more centered. "Come on."

They ran to the end of the building. Colby peered around the edge. No one…yet.

They took another sprint down another length of the building, and when Colby peered around that corner, which was the vantage point of the lab, he didn't see anyone. Both vehicles were sitting idle. He just hoped there were keys inside. He didn't want to have to take the time to hot-wire the car.

"We need to get low. Crawl. We have to stay under the windows."

They all got down on their hands and knees. The shrubs were dry and pokey, but he didn't hear one word of complaint from Regan or Olivia. They slithered forward to the closest Jeep, staying as near to the building as possible to keep from being spotted. Colby glanced up—the guard tower appeared empty.

They inched into the gap between the first and second Jeeps. They were convertible—with nothing that would shelter them from being seen. Roll bars did little to prevent getting shot. Colby reached up and fumbled for the ignition. He couldn't believe it. There was a key.

Colby turned back to Regan. "You're going to have to drive."

Regan nodded. He motioned for Olivia to crawl in and lie down in the back. He got in after her. Regan eased up into the driver's seat and turned the vehicle's engine over.

That was when a window broke and the gunfire started. Regan threw the Jeep into Reverse and stomped on the gas, causing Colby to fall forward against the dashboard. He grabbed his assault rifle and laid down suppressive fire toward the building until Regan could get them moving forward.

She braked hard. The car swiveled slightly as she threw it into gear. Colby braced so he could keep his position. Once they were moving, he grabbed the rocket launcher and loaded it. He stood, keeping his stance wide, and fired.

A direct hit to the other Jeep. At least they wouldn't follow them that way.

That was when he saw four men pour through the hole he'd also left in the side of the building.

All Regan could do was follow the worn route through the brush in front of her. There wasn't clearly a road but what appeared to be more of an old Jeep trail. Hadn't there been streets leading in and out of this facility?

Soon, her question was answered when they struck pavement.

"Olivia, are you okay?" Regan asked.

In the rearview mirror she saw Olivia's head pop up and her hand gave her a thumbs-up sign. She turned to Colby. "And you?"

He turned to her with a tentative smile. "Good but—"

And that was when they heard it, the thumping of the helicopter blades quickly closing in.

"That's what I was worried about."

He stood and faced backward, steadying himself against the roll bar. Regan heard what sounded like the worst hail storm ever closing the distance on their vehicle.

"Faster," Colby said.

Regan looked quickly behind her as he settled

the rocket launcher on his shoulder. She turned back around and that was when she saw the deer standing in the middle of the road. She veered to the left. A scream pealed from Olivia's lips, kicking Regan's heartbeat into a dizzying pace. Colby was knocked awkwardly over the passenger seat. She heard the ping of metal against metal.

Colby shot upright. "Step on it!"

Regan righted the vehicle and nearly stood on the gas, making the Jeep rear forward. The dirt puffed violently beside the vehicle in tiny explosions as it was blown apart by a spray of bullets. Regan's head throbbed. She gritted her teeth.

If their captors moved that gun a few inches to the right, she would feel those bullets rip through her body.

Regan heard the whistle, felt the heat of the rocket leaving the launcher, and then a faint hit of metal hitting metal.

The world burst bright and heat whooshed over Regan, her hair fanning forward from the concussive wave of the blast. An unseen hand forced their vehicle off the road and Regan's hands came off the wheel as Colby covered her body with his.

The Jeep eventually slowed. Colby squeezed tighter but Regan began to push him off in a fight for air.

He eased back, and she looked up, seeing trails of black smoke drift under the blue cloudless sky and shrapnel rain down.

"Is it over?" Olivia asked, crawling up from her place in the back.

Regan scanned Olivia and didn't see one drop of blood. She looked at Colby and brought her fingers up to his hair and face. "Were you hit?"

He grabbed her hands in his. "I'm fine. We're okay. I think that was the last of them."

"What now?"

"Just this."

He leaned forward and kissed her.

"Seriously?" Olivia cried out.

But then came the sound of another helicopter. Regan looked up and saw a military helicopter hovering over them. Ropes fanned out from either side and men rappelled down each one. Six in total.

"I think these are the good guys," Colby said.

The first man who landed on the ground took off his helmet.

It was Colby's friend, Nicholas Abrams.

TWENTY

For the first time in a long time, Colby was actually relieved to see Nico. Old feelings returned—the kinship kind and not the disappointment and anger he'd felt after their comrade's death. After everything he'd been through, perhaps he was ready to let bygones be bygones.

"Always late to the party," Colby said.

Nico smiled. "Always have to do everything on your own. Friends are here to help if you'll let them. And just FYI—we are a day earlier than planned."

"That's true. And the reason for your early arrival?"

"We used the chips you swallowed to find the compound. Once the helicopter flew in, we knew we better end things."

Colby reached out his hand and when Nico grabbed it, he pulled him into a quick hug. "Glad to see you here. By the way, what happened at the bank?"

"Turned out to be another interested party—not the good kind. We know Brian was trying to play several entities against one another to drive the price of his bioweapon up. Some of this information we found hidden in the lab on his personal property. We didn't know all the players, but the few we knew were definitely bad apples. The men that kept you here at the compound were private security hired by Brian until he could pick his ultimate winner." Nico spoke into his shoulder microphone, and the helicopter veered off in the direction of the compound. "Those guys will go back and secure the compound, though it looks like you handled the situation pretty well."

"There're still some stragglers back there," Colby said.

"They're prepared for that."

Colby looked back. Olivia was huddled next to her mom. Both alive and well, though a little worse for wear.

"What happens now?" Colby asked, keeping them in his sights.

Lord, please... I don't want to lose any more women in my life. People I love...

Was that true? Did he love Regan? Could love happen in a matter of days? Long-lasting love? Would he be blessed enough to find it twice in his lifetime?

"Colby." Nico pressed the toe of his boot into the dirt and started shuffling stones. He didn't… or maybe couldn't look at Colby. "It's Sam."

It was as if a sword pierced Colby's gut. In the days they'd been gone had something horrible happened to his sister?

Had the worst thing happened?

"What is it? Please—"

"She's alive, but sicker."

"We have to get Regan back. We put the cure somewhere safe. I can… You can go and get it—"

Nico raised a hand. "Colby, slow down. We recovered the polio virus. It wasn't too hard for us to track once we knew you were helping Regan. It's safely back at the hospital."

"Great. Then you can fly Regan straight to Sam…" Colby's voice trailed. Something in Nico's gaze twisted the invisible sword in his belly.

"I have to take her into custody, Colby. This is a national security concern. I'll see what I can do about getting her released, but the hospital is a different story. They may never let her touch a patient there again."

"Nico—" Colby placed his fist against his chest "—you can fix this. You have the power. You know what kind of duress she was under. She's got what you need as far as Brian's buyers.

That information alone should secure an immunity agreement for her."

"That's all true—but the hospital—that will be the challenge."

Nico walked away and approached Regan. After no more than five seconds her hands were to her face, her shoulders heaving. A few words Colby couldn't hear were exchanged between them, but the meaning was clear from Regan's body language.

Nico walked back to Colby. "She asking if you'll take Olivia…for now. Says you're the only one she trusts."

He nodded. Regan smiled weakly, and Olivia jumped out of the Jeep and straight into his arms.

Regan was tired, so tired. There was little to do but look at the four nondescript walls painted in beige. There was one mesh window in the steel door that locked her in this room.

From one prison to another. Things are not looking up for me.

They'd interrogated her for hours. Maybe *interrogation* was too harsh a word. Nico had been very matter-of-fact in his questioning. He was constantly back and forth from the room as if he was verifying Regan's story with what they'd found at the compound. Colby and

Olivia were questioned, as well, but they hadn't been detained.

For once, she didn't worry about Olivia. Regan knew she was safe with Colby. She was worried about Sam. About whether or not they'd let her try to save her life.

Lord, after everything Colby's done for me—please, have them release me. Please let the hospital allow me to perform Sam's surgery.

There was a microwaveable cup of macaroni and cheese sitting in front of her that had congealed long ago. The most her stomach could take was a few sips of water. At that moment, she began to understand something about faith. Only when she was in trouble did she think to turn to God. When things went well, she didn't sense a need for help. But here, in prison, when everything had been stripped away, it was the only thing she could think of.

Is it weird to feel almost thankful this happened? I learned that a man could want the best for me...could actually help me. That he could make me feel safe and not harmed. Olivia and I are closer than ever. I feel like God is with me.

That whatever happens will be okay—except for Sam. Lord, please, don't let Sam be collateral damage.

She leaned forward and remembered the picture she'd hastily tucked into her back pocket.

She pulled the page out, unfolded it, and traced her finger over the innocently penned lines Olivia had drawn.

A house. A man, woman and child off to one side. A tree. The sun with radiant beams. A rainbow. The figures clearly represented Colby, Regan and Olivia. The man stood between the woman and child, holding each of their hands. And then a heart—not drawn by Olivia but by Colby given the fluid assuredness of the line, surrounded all three figures.

Did that simply drawn heart mean he wanted what she did—to never be apart again?

There was a brisk knock at the door and Nicholas stepped in.

He sat in front of her. "Brian Hollis has confirmed every bit of your story. We found the notebook you mentioned still on him. Thankfully, the contents of the lab survived the explosion when Colby blew up their spare vehicle. Brian basically gave a full confession to everything. To coercing you into stealing the virus. To killing Polina. To kidnapping you and Colby."

"And what did he get for that?"

"Let's just say he won't see the light of day again, but he'll live. Sometimes life, even in prison, is worth bargaining for."

"So what now?" Regan asked.

"We're going to release you."

"What about the hospital?"

Abrams folded his hands in front of her. "Without disclosing too much, I made contact with your hospital CEO, chief of medicine and chief of surgery. I explained that you'd been very helpful in thwarting several probable terrorist attacks much at the risk to your own life. That you should be viewed as a hero…or heroine, I guess."

"But is that truc?"

Nicholas leaned forward. "Regan, heroes are made not because they always make the right choices, but in how they finish. Your actions are understandable considering the pressure you were under. You never put any lives in danger, but were willing to sacrifice yourself to keep Brian from accomplishing what he wanted. That is heroism."

"What about the notebooks?"

"We have them. They'll be locked away."

"I want them destroyed. I don't want anyone to see the early versions of my work—whatever happened that led to those deaths."

Nicholas slid one hand forward. "Regan, Brian confessed to manipulating your early experiments. He just really needed to find the jumping-off point from where he started. That's why he allowed you to get your journals. It surprised him that you still had thcm. Hc couldn't remember the right version he'd manipulated. What you have in those notebooks is benign. Trust me. I've had our best microbiologists review them."

For the first time in a long time, Regan felt like she could breathe again.

"First, I need to go to the hospital to check on Colby's sister."

"Of course."

Regan was escorted out of the building. Nicholas pointed off to the side, where Colby waited with Olivia. She approached them, and Colby's arms swallowed her, and she was safe and whole again.

"Let's go save Sam," Regan said.

Colby's hands smoothed up her back and settled on top of her shoulders. He eased her back from his embrace and locked his eyes with hers. "I need to say something to you."

Regan's heart thumped at the base of her throat. She swallowed to try to chase it away without success. It was hard to read the look in Colby's eyes. *What is he going to say? Did I misinterpret the feelings I thought he had for me? Is this the easy letdown?*

"I want to be sure you understand something. It's important to me that you hear these words before you see Sam."

Regan pressed her lips together to keep them from trembling. She would die right here if he didn't get to the words soon, but so was fear seizing her chest at what those words might be.

"Regan Lockhart—I love you. I love Olivia."

Tears brimmed Regan's eyes and Colby pulled her tightly against him.

"I love you, too," Regan said.

His chest heaved underneath her and he squeezed her tighter.

"I know that you'll do all you can to save Sam and she still might die. I need you to hear, right now, that I will not blame you if that happens."

Regan pressed into him, unable to stem the flow of tears. He gripped her tightly in a one-arm embrace and then tipped her chin up as he gently pressed his lips against hers.

What she hoped for was realized.

"I'll always be with you," Colby said.

And it was the first promise from a man that Regan believed with everything in her.

EPILOGUE

Nine months later

Regan clutched Olivia's hand in hers as they stood on Sam's parents' front porch. It was a day she'd hoped against hope would come.

A party for Sam to celebrate her remission. Regan's cure had saved Sam's life.

The door flew open and Sam piled out, enveloping Regan in a breath-halting hug. Regan encircled Sam with her arms, laughing, returning the embrace. "You get stronger every time I see you."

Sam eased her back. "Can you believe it! Another clear scan? The tumor just melted away like you said it would."

The physician in Regan wanted to temper Sam's expectations, but today was not a day to do that.

Regan reached her hand out and laid it against Sam's cheek, feeling tears brim her eyelids. "You are so beautiful." And Sam was, truly. Her hair had grown back. Her cheeks were vibrant with a hint of rosy pink. Her smile was infectious—the good kind.

"Well, don't keep standing there. Come inside. Someone's waiting for you."

Regan's fingers tingled.

Olivia skipped into the house. "Colby!" she yelled.

"In the backyard," Regan heard his voice call out.

When she'd been released by the military, she and Colby had raced to the hospital only to find Sam in what could be called a very bad state of affairs. The seizures had taken such hold that the medical team had put her in a drug-induced coma to keep them at bay. She'd been heavily sedated and on a breathing machine. The medical team had scanned her that morning and the tumor had grown—over the point where Regan thought the virus could actually work.

Against the hospital's wishes, Regan had decided to go ahead with the procedure.

After infusing the virus, the inflammatory response her body mounted was impressive and, though the tumor was dying, the immune reaction was causing significant swelling in Sam's brain. At one point, Regan thought there'd be little chance Sam would make it.

But every day, Regan would spend time with Colby at Sam's bedside. All Regan could do medically was done. So they would pray—for hours on end—for Sam to wake up.

And she did. Though the road was hard, she'd come through it.

Sometimes illness was the glue that held people together, and Regan worried that had become the case with her and Colby, but once Sam was on the path to recovery they hit an easy stride and found that they truly were connected in every meaningful way.

And, most importantly, Olivia loved Colby—maybe more than Regan did, if that were possible.

Regan wove through Sam's parents' house. It wasn't the first time she'd been there, but things were amiss.

Sam hovered playfully behind her, giggling every now and then.

Regan turned around. "I thought we were celebrating?"

"We are—just not me. We're celebrating you and..."

Regan laughed. "Sam, seriously. What is going on?"

The French doors opened and there stood Colby underneath an archway of summer flowers. Sam's family stood off to the side—these people she'd grown to love and cherish over the past several months. People she felt were the family she'd never had.

Colby's sapphire-blue eyes held hers, and she felt herself magnetically drawn like a compass needle to true north. His smile was broad, disarming. She felt haltingly smitten by the jeans, white pressed shirt and brown sport coat he wore.

He held his hand out to her. "Regan, I need you to come closer. I have a question."

Truly, she felt weak in the knees. Olivia grabbed her hand and started to pull her forward. Regan wanted to slow this moment down, to remember the twinkle in his eyes. His creased laugh lines. His dimples.

Regan drew closer and Colby held his hand out to her and grabbed the ends of her fingertips. "Regan Lockhart, never have I loved someone more than you. You saved my sister's life. You saved…my life. With you I learned it was possible to love someone wholly again. Regan, will you marry me?"

Tears streamed down Regan's face and she trembled. Olivia tugged at her hand.

"Can we give it to him now?" Olivia pleaded.

Regan shook her head and pulled out a small envelope she'd kept in her pocket for the last three months, hoping that someday this moment would come.

Regan held it forward with trembling fingers. “This is our answer.”

Colby released her hand. He opened the envelope and withdrew the bracelet. It was heavy, made of gold. On the band was an engraving of the photo he and Olivia had drawn together.

He looked at Regan, his eyes glistening.

“Read the back!” Olivia yelled.

Colby laughed and turned the bracelet over.

Regan envisioned what his eyes were seeing. “We say yes.”

Colby pulled her into a tight embrace, and Olivia wrapped her arms around both of them.

“It’s perfect,” Colby said. Then he pulled away and raised his hands above his head, pumping his fists in the air. “They said yes!”

* * * * *

If you enjoyed TAKEN HOSTAGE,
look for FRACTURED MEMORY
by Jordyn Redwood.

Dear Reader,

Taken Hostage was inspired by two true medical stories I found very interesting.

Duke University Medical Center is actually in phase I clinical trials using a genetically modified poliovirus that is working in some patients to cure recurrent glioblastoma. Of course, the leap that a cure like this could be further manipulated into a bioweapon is (as far as I know) fiction.

The second was based on Italian physician Dr. Paolo Macchiarini who specializes in building tracheas (or windpipes). He is considered a maverick, but also some patients' last hope at life. His compassion struck me after I watched a documentary called *A Leap of Faith: A Meredith Vieira Special*. What if this man went missing?

To what lengths would I go to find him if it was my loved one that needed him?

I always LOVE to hear from readers and can be reached via email at jordyn@jordynredwood.com or by mail at the following address: Jordyn Redwood, PO Box 1142, Parker, Colorado 80134.

Many Blessings,
Jordyn